25 FEB 2017

TM

0 2 NOV 2013

7/13

© 1995-2013 Nintendo/Creatures Inc./GAME FREAK inc.
TM and ® and character names are trademarks of Nintendo.
POCKET MONSTER SPECIAL (Magazine Edition)
by Hidenori KUSAKA, Satoshi YAMAMOTO
© 1997 Hidenori KUSAKA, Satoshi YAMAMOTO
All rights reserved.
Original Japanese edition published by SHOGAKUKAN.
English translation rights in the United States of America, Canada,
the United Kingdom and Ireland arranged with SHOGAKUKAN.

English Adaptation / Bryant Turnage
Translation / Tetsuichiro Miyaki
Touch-up & Lettering / Susan Daigle-Leach
Design / Fawn Lau
Editor / Annette Roman

Printed in the U.S.A.

Published by VIZ Media, LLC
P.O. Box 77010
San Francisco, CA 94107

10 9 8 7 6 5 4 3 2 1
First printing, June 2013

www.vizkids.com

www.viz.com

PARENTAL ADVISORY
POKÉMON ADVENTURES
is rated A and is suitable
for readers of all ages.
ratings.viz.com

POKÉMON™

BLACK AND WHITE

VOL. 10

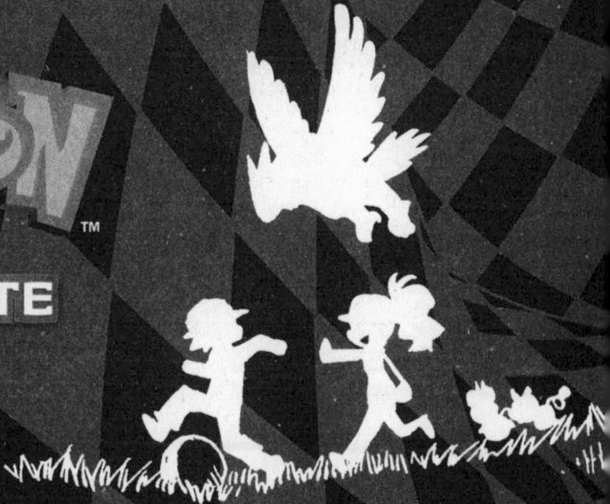

THE STORY THUS FAR!

Pokémon Trainer Black is exploring the mysterious Unova region with his brand-new Pokédex. Pokémon Trainer White runs a thriving talent agency for performing Pokémon. While traveling together, their paths cross with Team Plasma, a nefarious group that advocates releasing your Pokémon into the wild! Now Black and White are off on their own separate journeys of discovery...

BLACK'S dream is to win the Pokémon League!

WHITE'S dream is to make her Tepig Gigi a star!

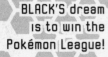

Black's Munna, MUSHA, helps him think clearly by temporarily "eating" his dream.

White's Tepig, GIGI, and Black's Pignite, NITE, get along like peanut butter and jelly! But now Gigi has left White for another Trainer...

Adventure ㉜
Mine Mayhem

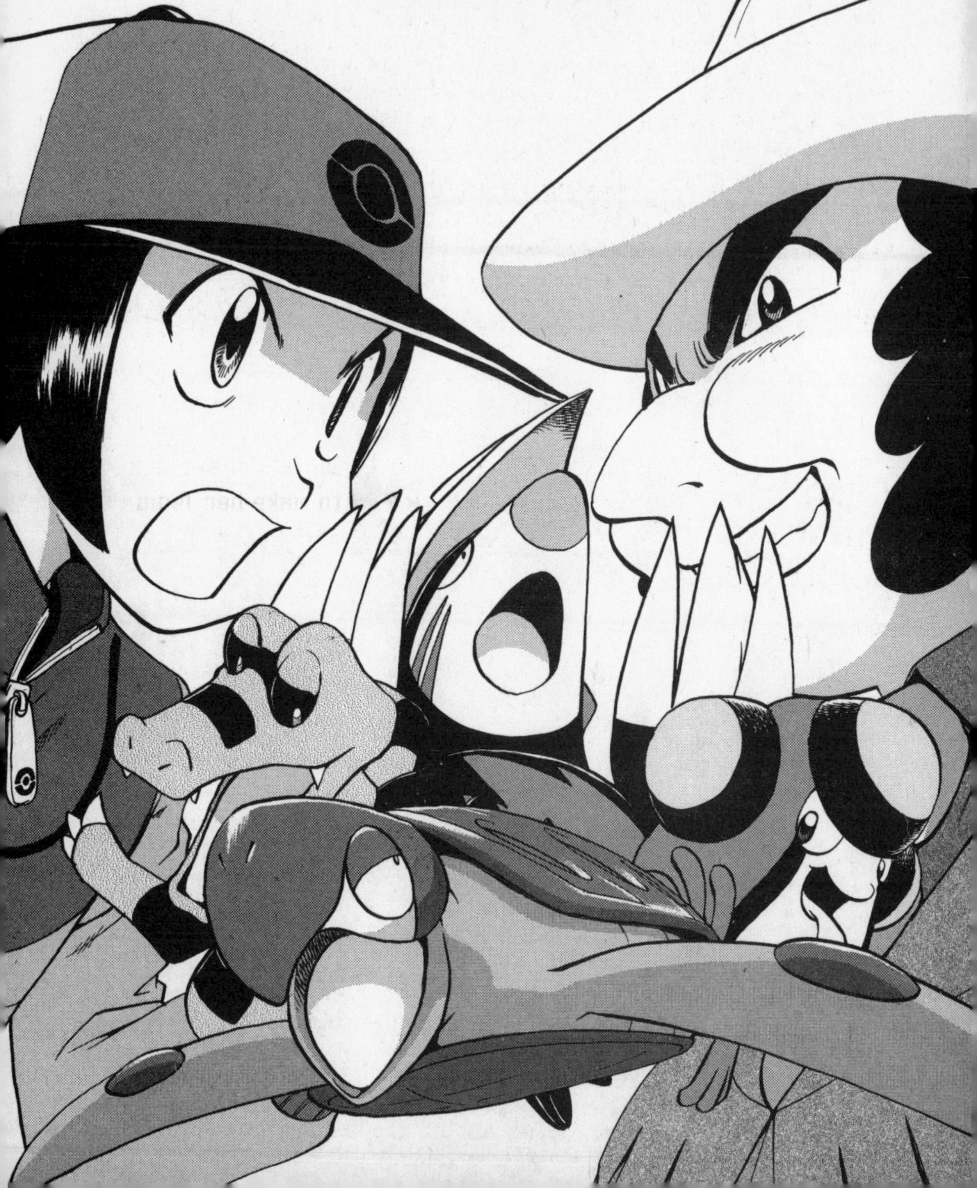

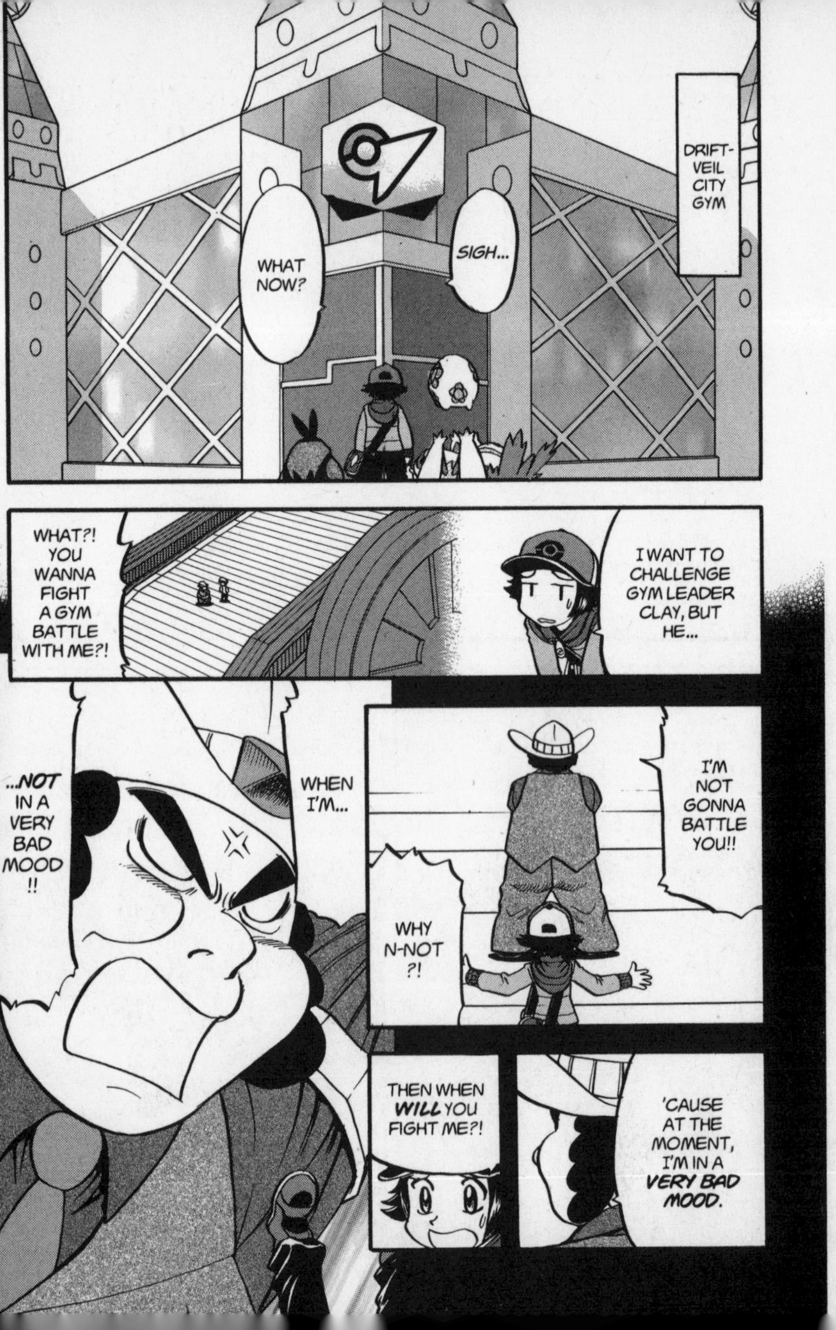
DRIFT-VEIL CITY GYM
SIGH...
WHAT NOW?
I WANT TO CHALLENGE GYM LEADER CLAY, BUT HE...
WHAT?! YOU WANNA FIGHT A GYM BATTLE WITH ME?!
I'M NOT GONNA BATTLE YOU!!
WHY N-NOT?!
'CAUSE AT THE MOMENT, I'M IN A **VERY BAD MOOD.**
THEN WHEN **WILL** YOU FIGHT ME?!
WHEN I'M...
...**NOT** IN A VERY BAD MOOD!!

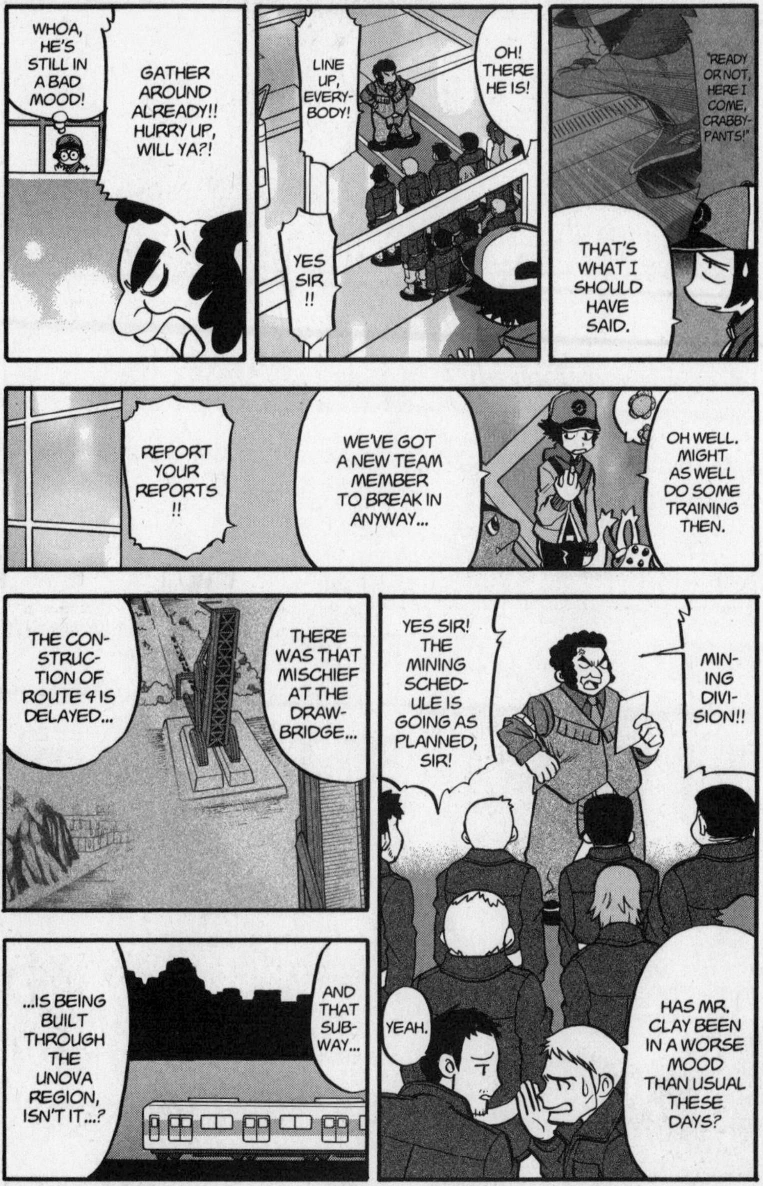
"READY OR NOT, HERE I COME, CRABBY-PANTS!"
THAT'S WHAT I SHOULD HAVE SAID.
OH! THERE HE IS!
LINE UP, EVERYBODY!
YES SIR!!
GATHER AROUND ALREADY!! HURRY UP, WILL YA?!
WHOA, HE'S STILL IN A BAD MOOD!
OH WELL. MIGHT AS WELL DO SOME TRAINING THEN.
WE'VE GOT A NEW TEAM MEMBER TO BREAK IN ANYWAY...
REPORT YOUR REPORTS!!
MINING DIVISION!!
YES SIR! THE MINING SCHEDULE IS GOING AS PLANNED, SIR!
HAS MR. CLAY BEEN IN A WORSE MOOD THAN USUAL THESE DAYS?
YEAH.
THERE WAS THAT MISCHIEF AT THE DRAWBRIDGE...
THE CONSTRUCTION OF ROUTE 4 IS DELAYED...
AND THAT SUBWAY...
...IS BEING BUILT THROUGH THE UNOVA REGION, ISN'T IT...?

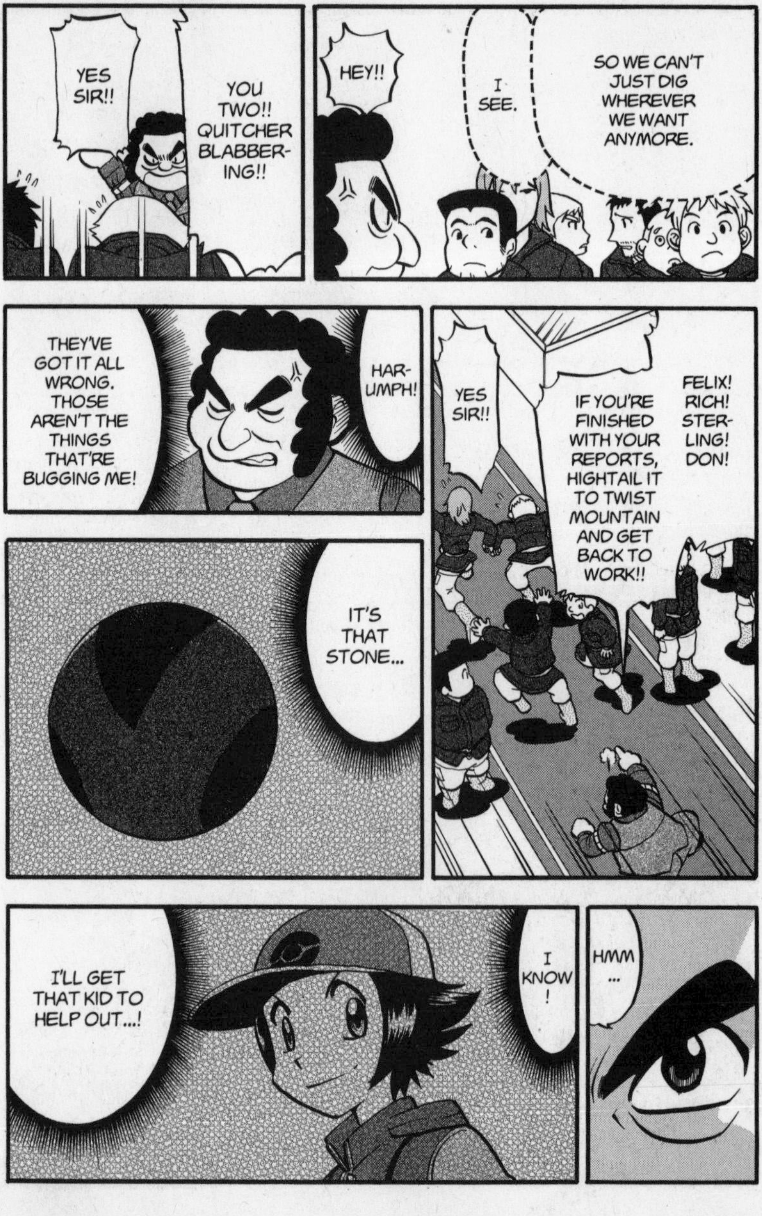
SO WE CAN'T JUST DIG WHEREVER WE WANT ANYMORE.
I SEE.
HEY!!
YOU TWO!! QUITCHER BLABBER-ING!!
YES SIR!!
FELIX! RICH! STER-LING! DON!
IF YOU'RE FINISHED WITH YOUR REPORTS, HIGHTAIL IT TO TWIST MOUNTAIN AND GET BACK TO WORK!!
YES SIR!!
HAR-UMPH!
THEY'VE GOT IT ALL WRONG. THOSE AREN'T THE THINGS THAT'RE BUGGING ME!
IT'S THAT STONE...
HMM ...
I KNOW !
I'LL GET THAT KID TO HELP OUT...!

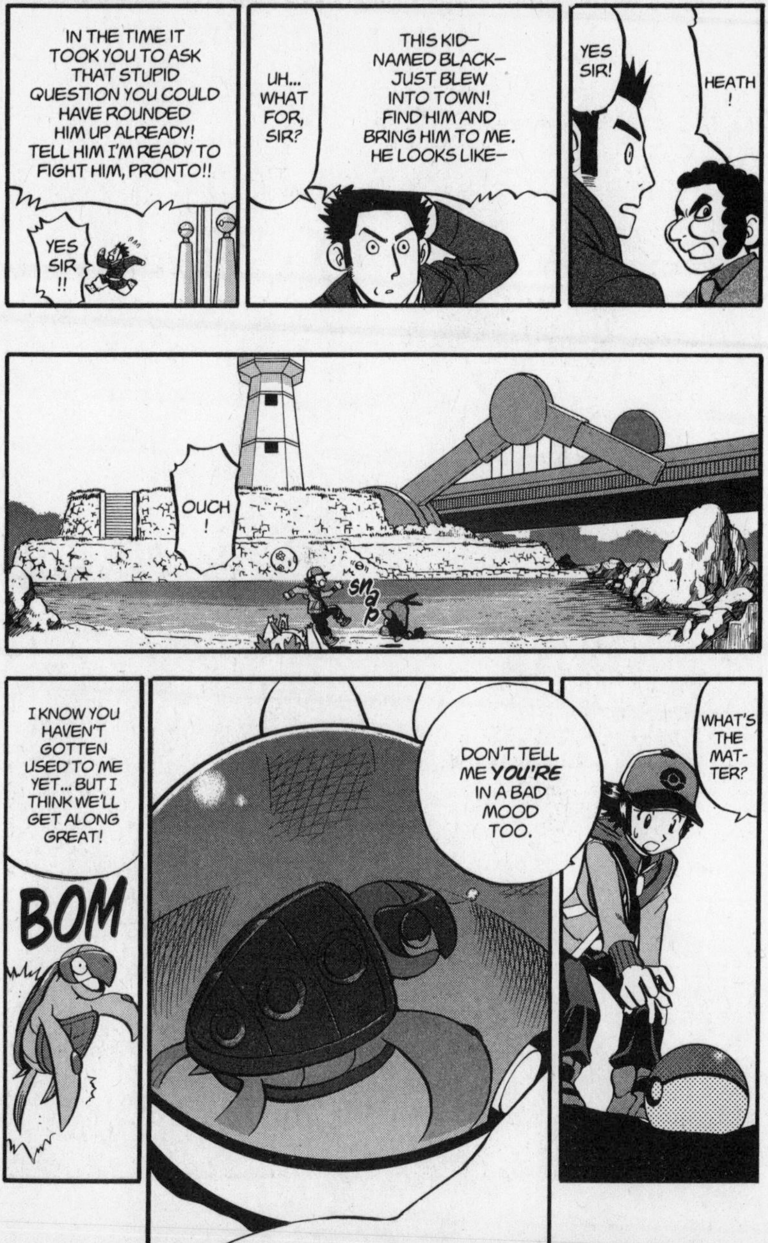
HEATH!
YES SIR!
THIS KID—NAMED BLACK—JUST BLEW INTO TOWN! FIND HIM AND BRING HIM TO ME. HE LOOKS LIKE—
UH... WHAT FOR, SIR?
IN THE TIME IT TOOK YOU TO ASK THAT STUPID QUESTION YOU COULD HAVE ROUNDED HIM UP ALREADY! TELL HIM I'M READY TO FIGHT HIM, PRONTO!!
YES SIR!!
OUCH!
SNAP
WHAT'S THE MATTER?
DON'T TELL ME ***YOU'RE*** IN A BAD MOOD TOO.
I KNOW YOU HAVEN'T GOTTEN USED TO ME YET... BUT I THINK WE'LL GET ALONG GREAT!
BOM

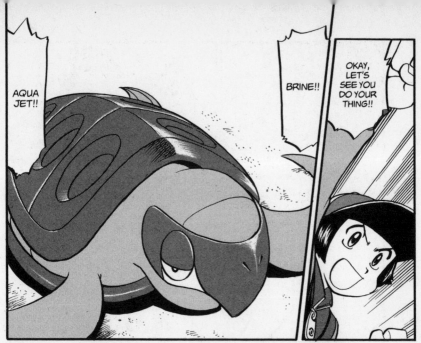

AQUA JET!!

BRINE!!

OKAY, LET'S SEE YOU DO YOUR THING!!

HUH?!

IT'S NOT WORKING. YOU WON'T LISTEN TO ME.

...

sploosh   sploosh

AAH!!

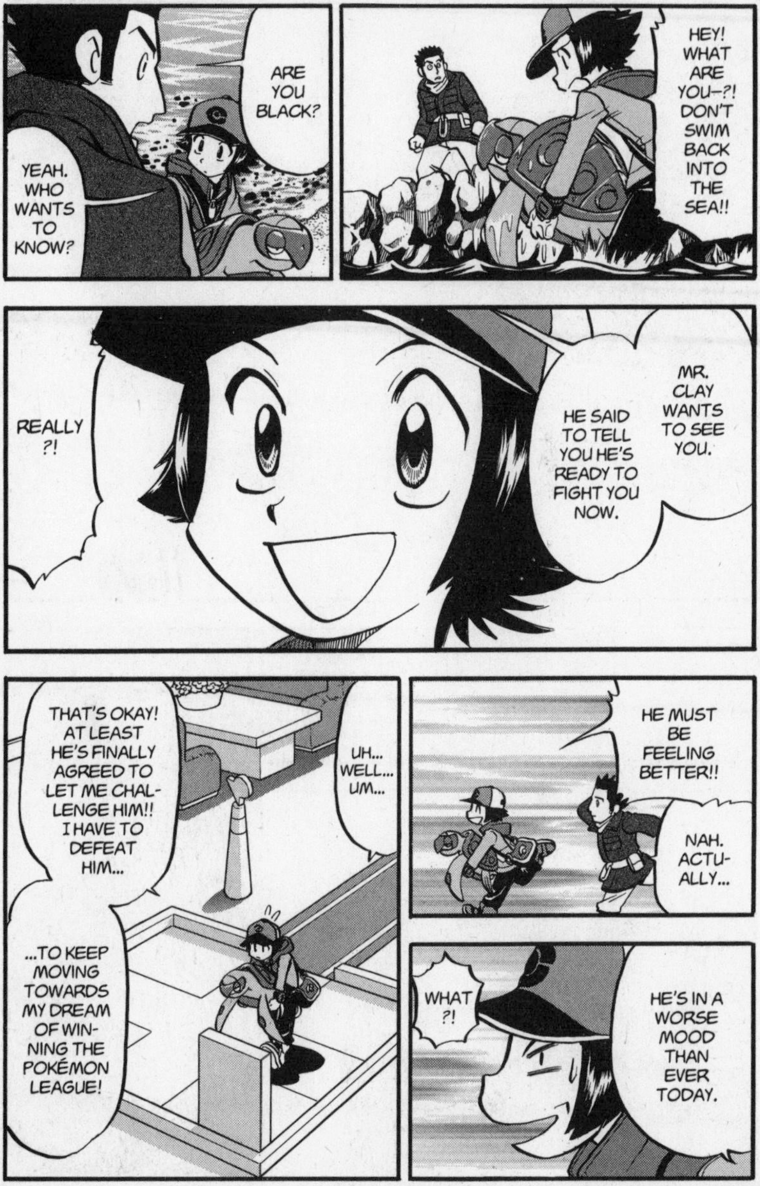
HEY! WHAT ARE YOU–?! DON'T SWIM BACK INTO THE SEA!!
ARE YOU BLACK?
YEAH. WHO WANTS TO KNOW?
MR. CLAY WANTS TO SEE YOU.
HE SAID TO TELL YOU HE'S READY TO FIGHT YOU NOW.
REALLY?!
HE MUST BE FEELING BETTER!!
NAH. ACTUALLY...
HE'S IN A WORSE MOOD THAN EVER TODAY.
WHAT?!
UH... WELL... UM...
THAT'S OKAY! AT LEAST HE'S FINALLY AGREED TO LET ME CHALLENGE HIM!! I HAVE TO DEFEAT HIM...
...TO KEEP MOVING TOWARDS MY DREAM OF WINNING THE POKÉMON LEAGUE!

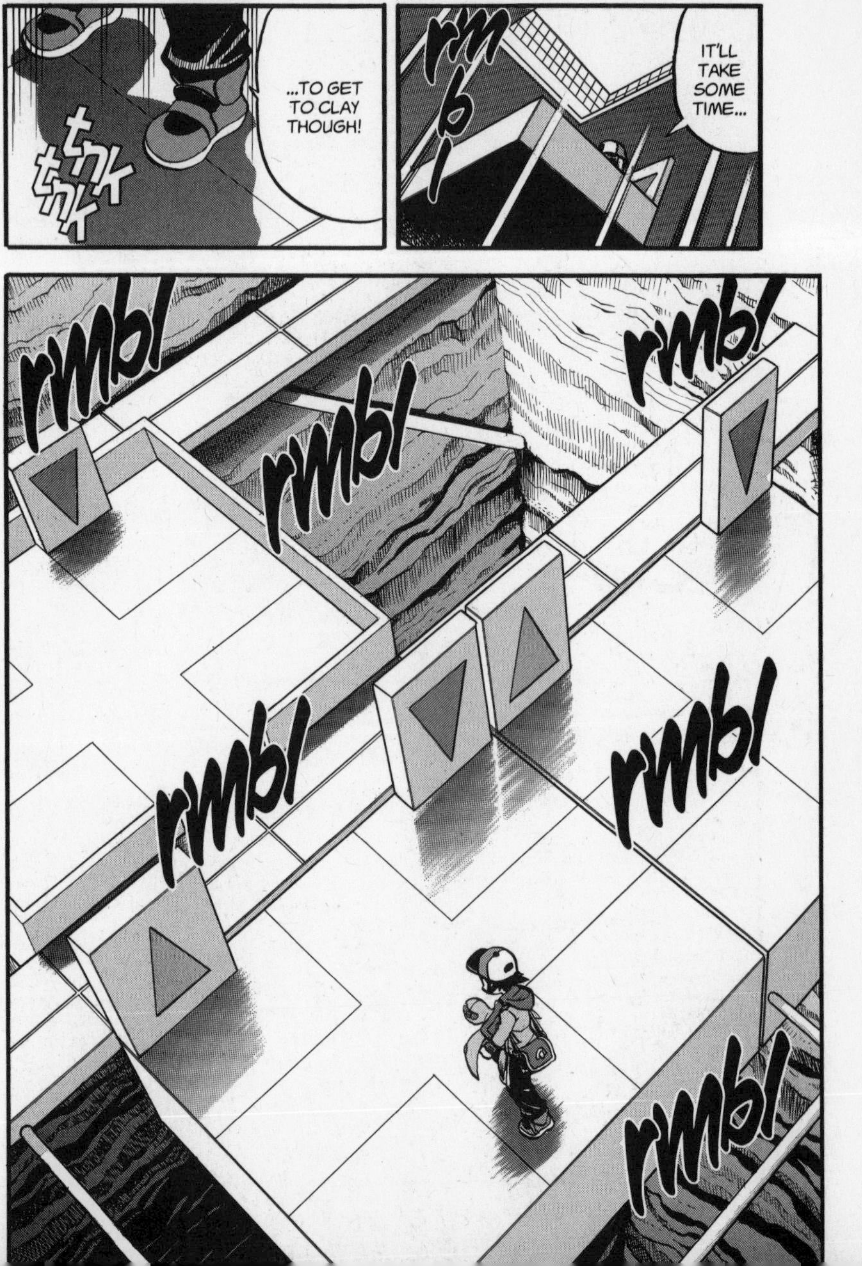
IT'LL TAKE SOME TIME...
r'mbl
...TO GET TO CLAY THOUGH!
r'mbl
r'mbl
r'mbl
r'mbl
r'mbl
r'mbl
r'mbl

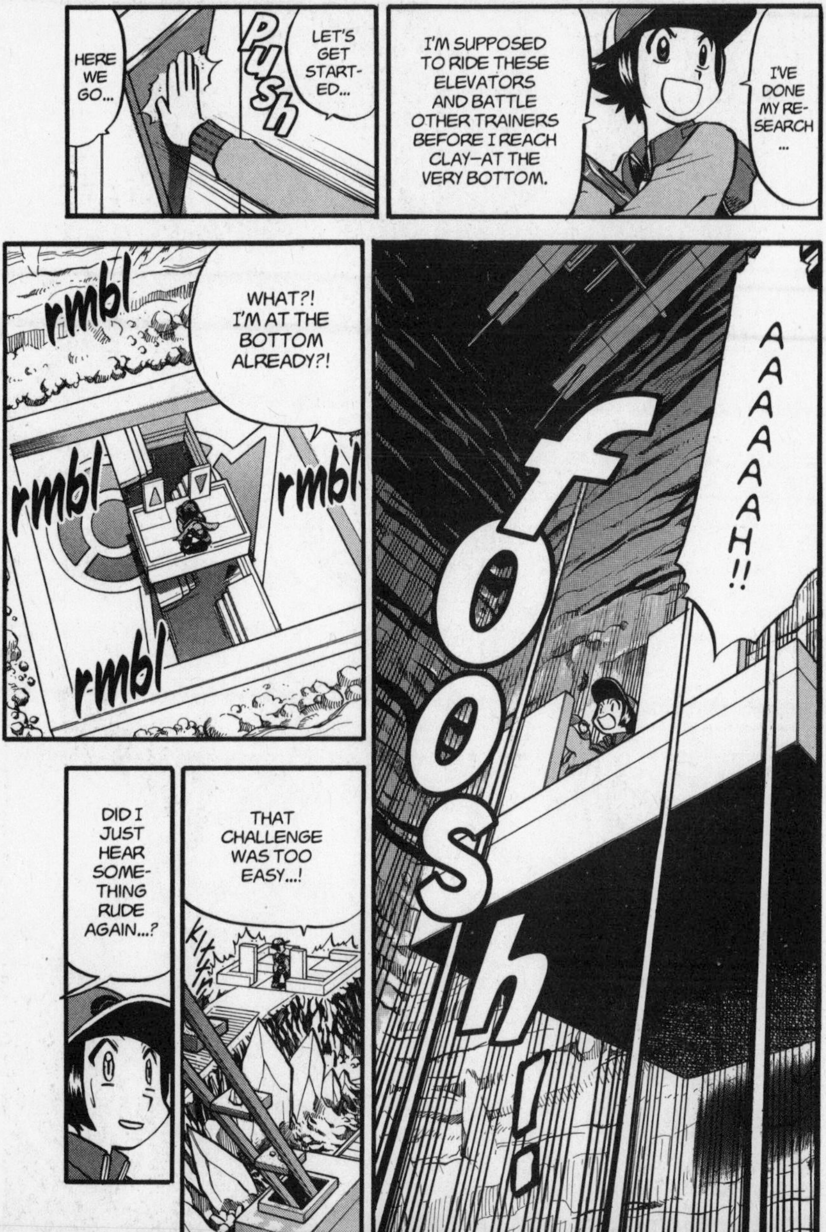
I'VE DONE MY RE-SEARCH ...
I'M SUPPOSED TO RIDE THESE ELEVATORS AND BATTLE OTHER TRAINERS BEFORE I REACH CLAY—AT THE VERY BOTTOM.
LET'S GET START-ED...
Push
HERE WE GO...
AAAAAAAH!!
foosh!
WHAT?! I'M AT THE BOTTOM ALREADY?!
rmbl
rmbl
rmbl
rmbl
THAT CHALLENGE WAS TOO EASY...!
DID I JUST HEAR SOME-THING RUDE AGAIN...?

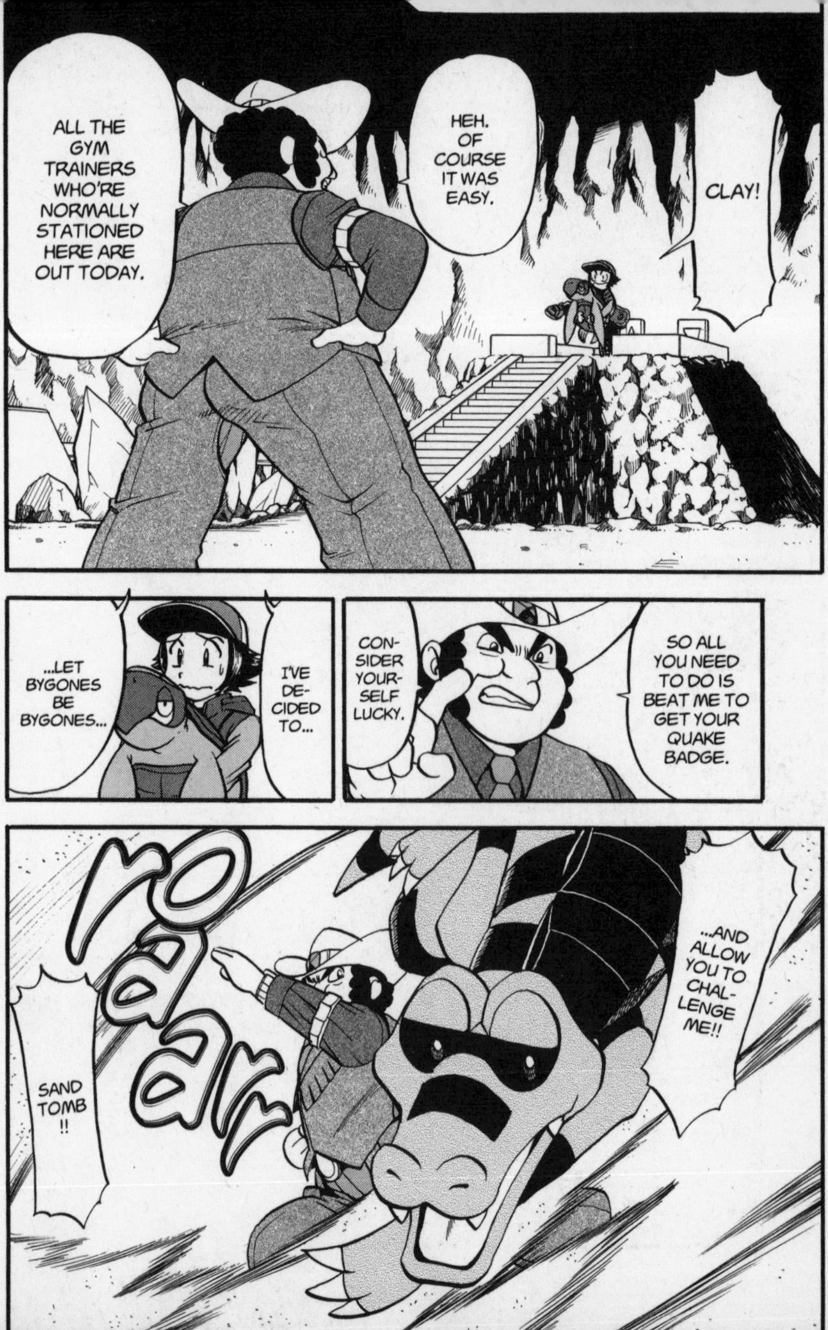
CLAY!
HEH. OF COURSE IT WAS EASY.
ALL THE GYM TRAINERS WHO'RE NORMALLY STATIONED HERE ARE OUT TODAY.
SO ALL YOU NEED TO DO IS BEAT ME TO GET YOUR QUAKE BADGE.
CON-SIDER YOUR-SELF LUCKY.
I'VE DE-CIDED TO...
...LET BYGONES BE BYGONES...
...AND ALLOW YOU TO CHAL-LENGE ME!!
roaar
SAND TOMB !!

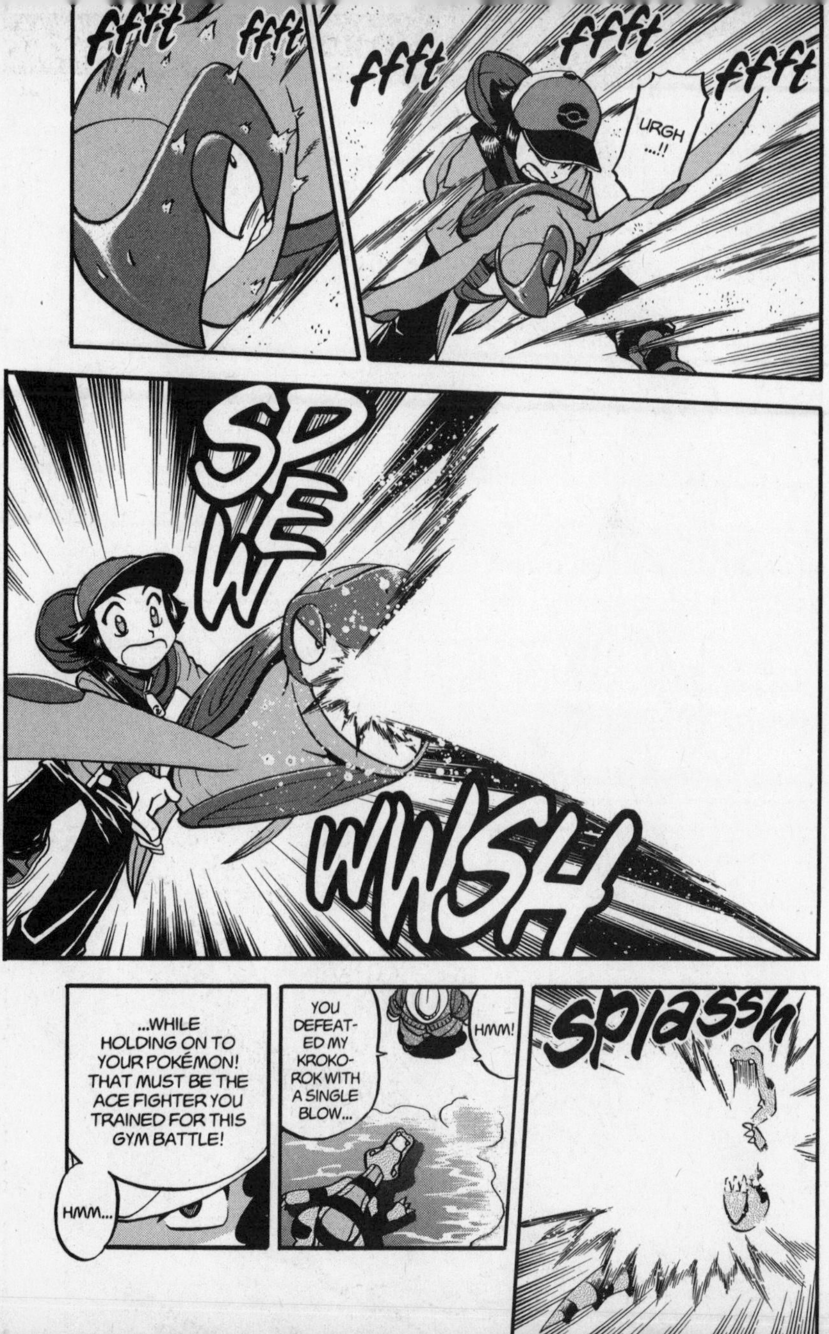
ffft
ffft
URGH ...!!
ffft
ffft
SPEW
WWSH
splassh
HMM!
YOU DEFEAT-ED MY KROKO-ROK WITH A SINGLE BLOW...
...WHILE HOLDING ON TO YOUR POKÉMON! THAT MUST BE THE ACE FIGHTER YOU TRAINED FOR THIS GYM BATTLE!
HMM...

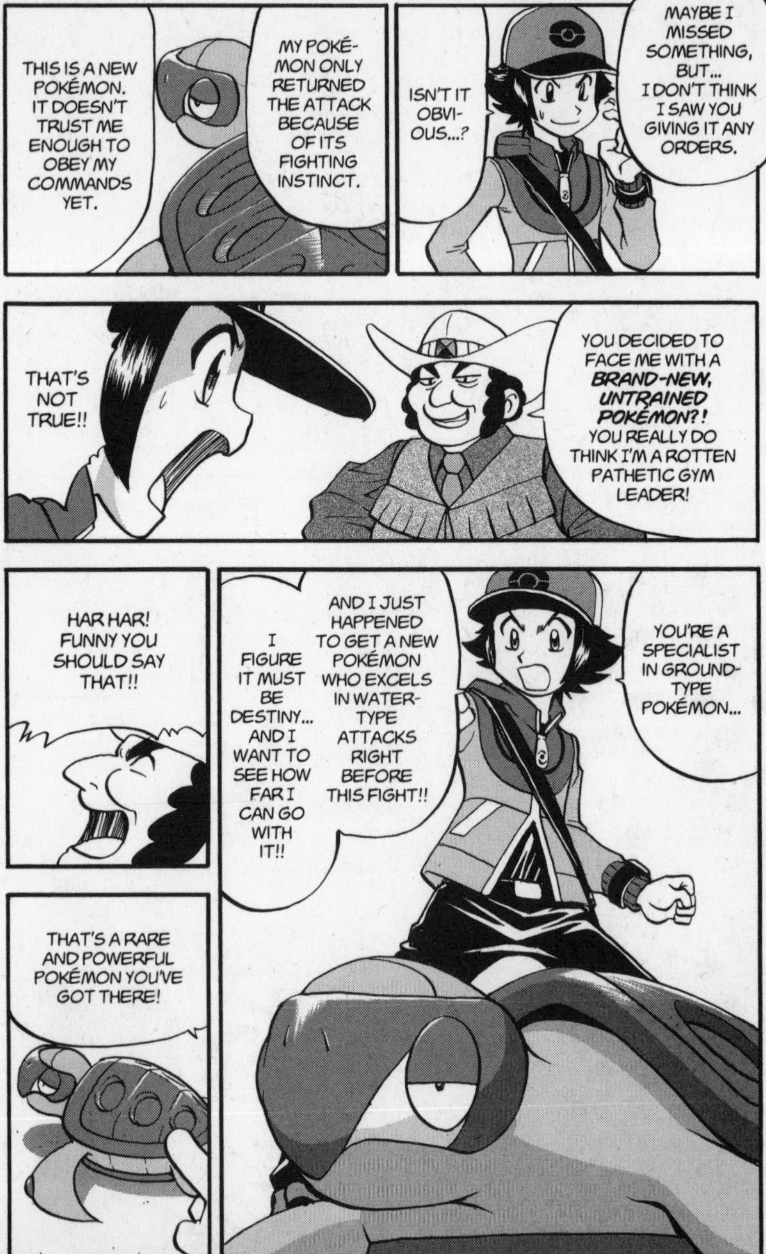
MAYBE I MISSED SOMETHING, BUT... I DON'T THINK I SAW YOU GIVING IT ANY ORDERS.
ISN'T IT OBVI-OUS...?
MY POKÉ-MON ONLY RETURNED THE ATTACK BECAUSE OF ITS FIGHTING INSTINCT.
THIS IS A NEW POKÉMON. IT DOESN'T TRUST ME ENOUGH TO OBEY MY COMMANDS YET.
YOU DECIDED TO FACE ME WITH A **BRAND-NEW, UNTRAINED POKÉMON?!** YOU REALLY DO THINK I'M A ROTTEN PATHETIC GYM LEADER!
THAT'S NOT TRUE!!
YOU'RE A SPECIALIST IN GROUND-TYPE POKÉMON...
AND I JUST HAPPENED TO GET A NEW POKÉMON WHO EXCELS IN WATER-TYPE ATTACKS RIGHT BEFORE THIS FIGHT!!
I FIGURE IT MUST BE DESTINY... AND I WANT TO SEE HOW FAR I CAN GO WITH IT!!
HAR HAR! FUNNY YOU SHOULD SAY THAT!!
THAT'S A RARE AND POWERFUL POKÉMON YOU'VE GOT THERE!

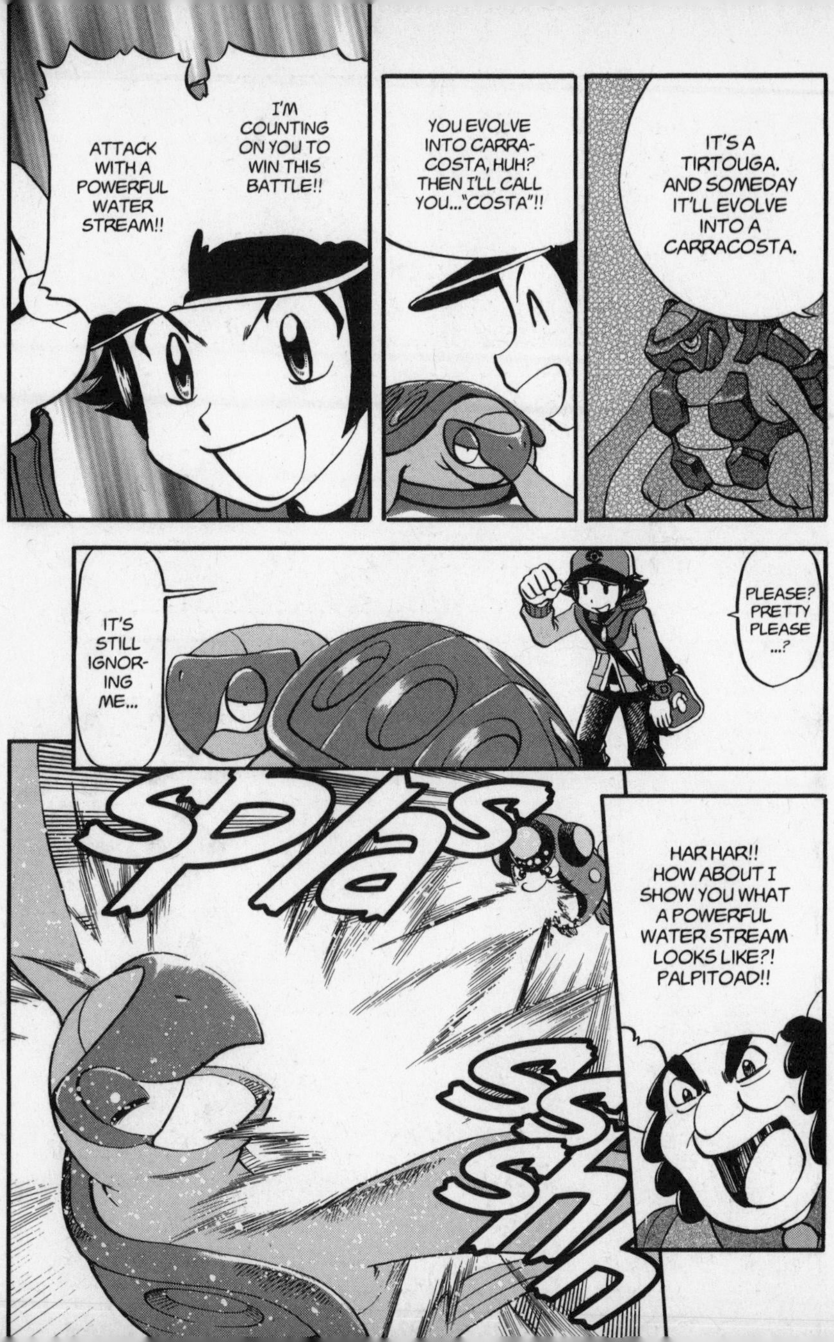
IT'S A TIRTOUGA. AND SOMEDAY IT'LL EVOLVE INTO A CARRACOSTA.
YOU EVOLVE INTO CARRA-COSTA, HUH? THEN I'LL CALL YOU..."COSTA"!!
I'M COUNTING ON YOU TO WIN THIS BATTLE!!
ATTACK WITH A POWERFUL WATER STREAM!!
PLEASE? PRETTY PLEASE ...?
IT'S STILL IGNORING-ING ME...
HAR HAR!! HOW ABOUT I SHOW YOU WHAT A POWERFUL WATER STREAM LOOKS LIKE?! PALPITOAD!!
splasssh

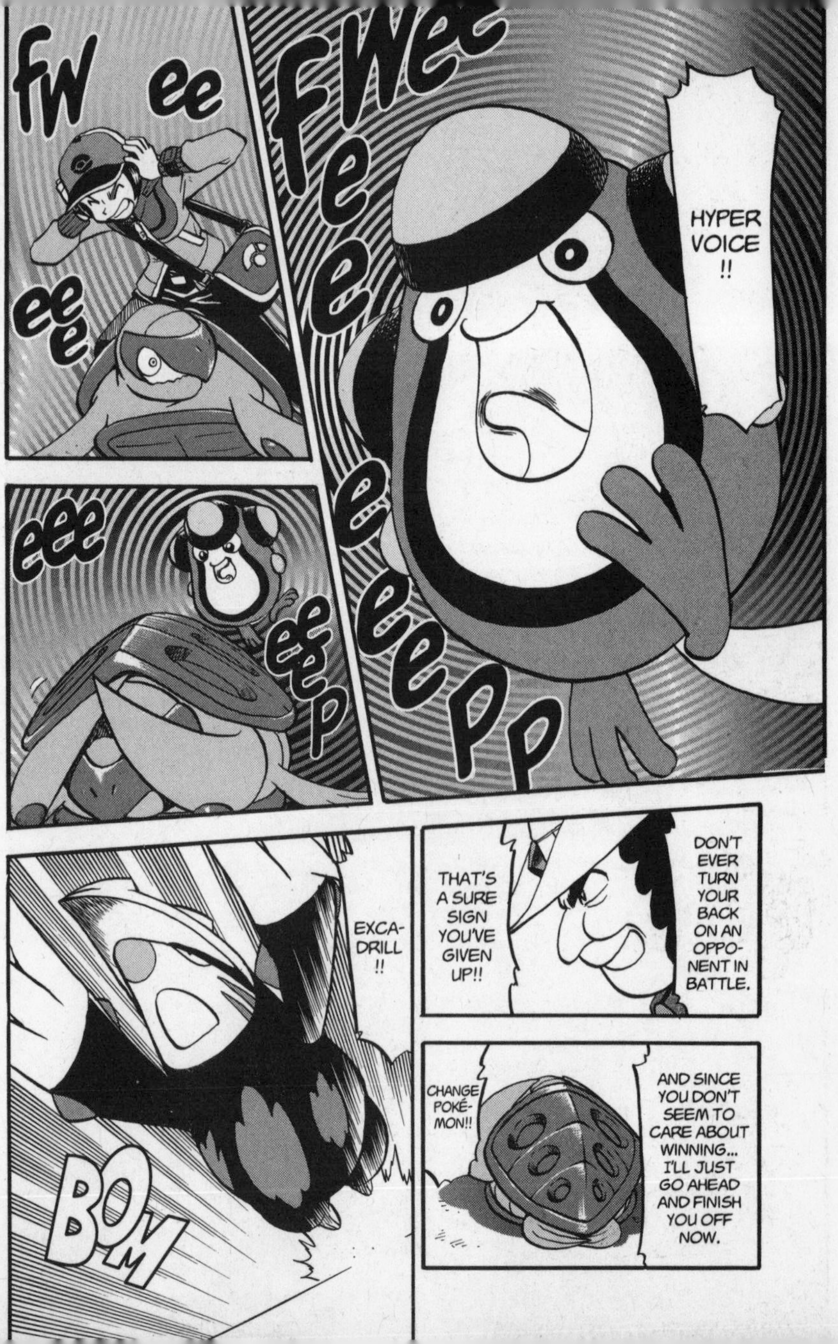
HYPER VOICE!!
FWEEEEEEEEPP
FWEEEEE
EEEEEEP
DON'T EVER TURN YOUR BACK ON AN OPPONENT IN BATTLE.
THAT'S A SURE SIGN YOU'VE GIVEN UP!!
AND SINCE YOU DON'T SEEM TO CARE ABOUT WINNING... I'LL JUST GO AHEAD AND FINISH YOU OFF NOW.
CHANGE POKÉMON!!
EXCADRILL!!
BOOM

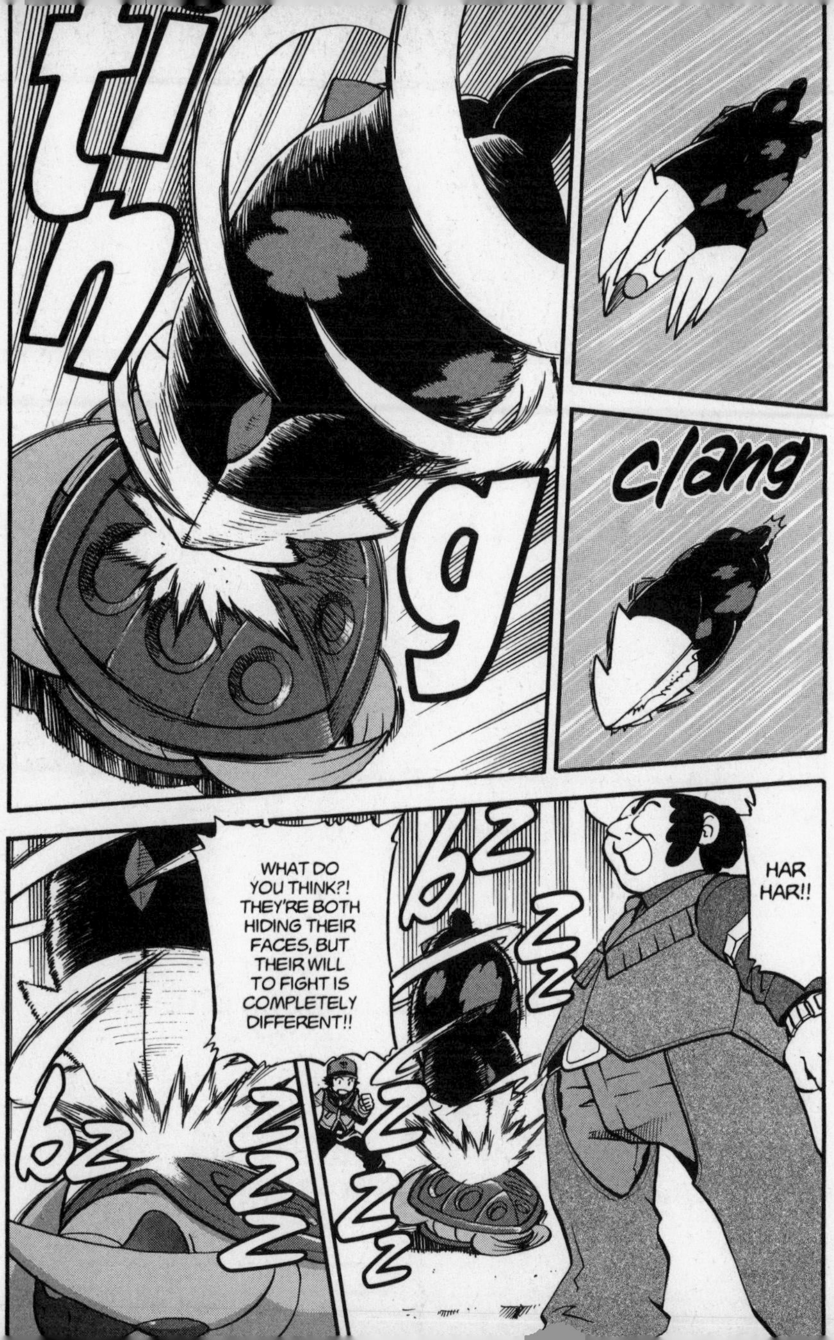
clang
ting
HAR HAR!!
WHAT DO YOU THINK?! THEY'RE BOTH HIDING THEIR FACES, BUT THEIR WILL TO FIGHT IS COMPLETELY DIFFERENT!!
bzzz
bzzzz
bzzzz

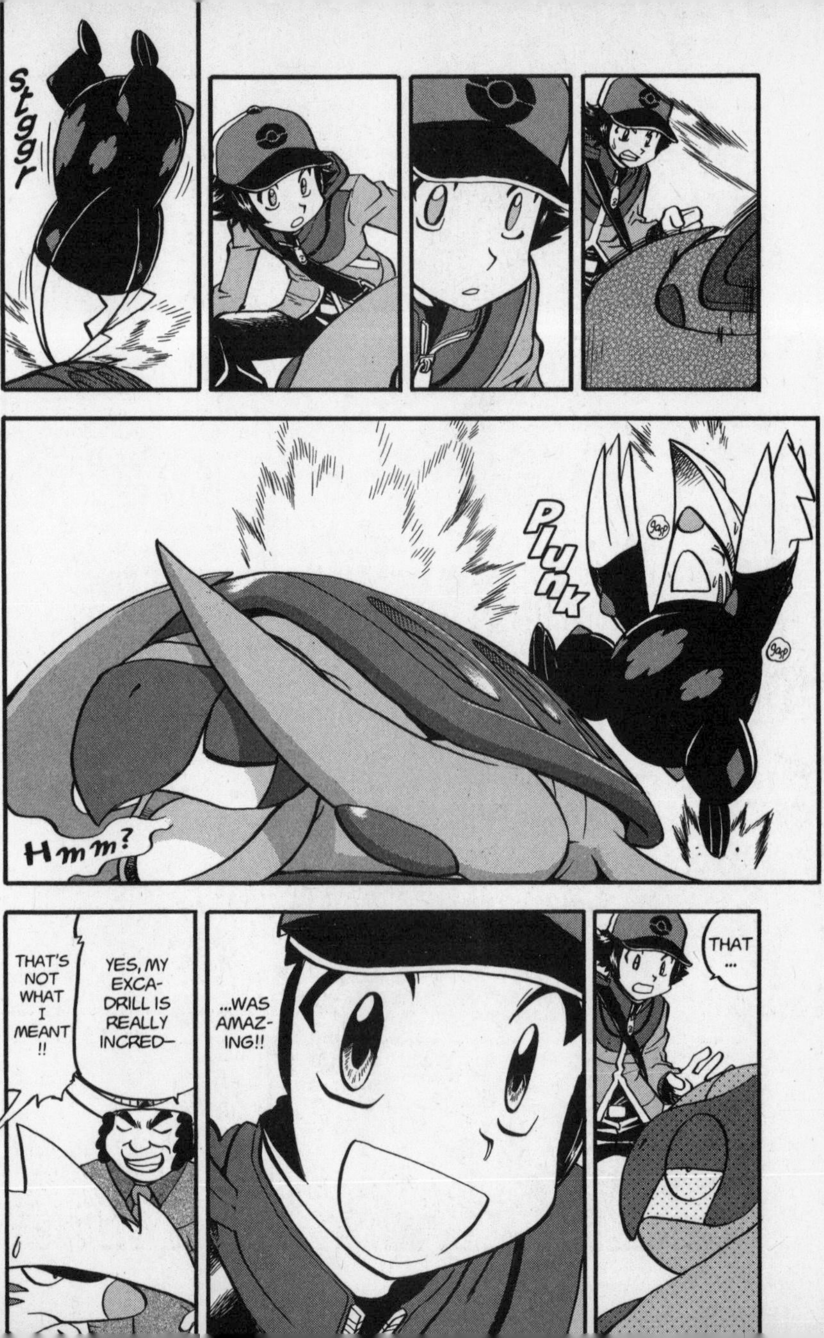
Stggr
gasp
Piunk
gasp
Hmmm?
THAT ...
...WAS AMAZING!!
YES, MY EXCA-DRILL IS REALLY INCRED-
THAT'S NOT WHAT I MEANT!!

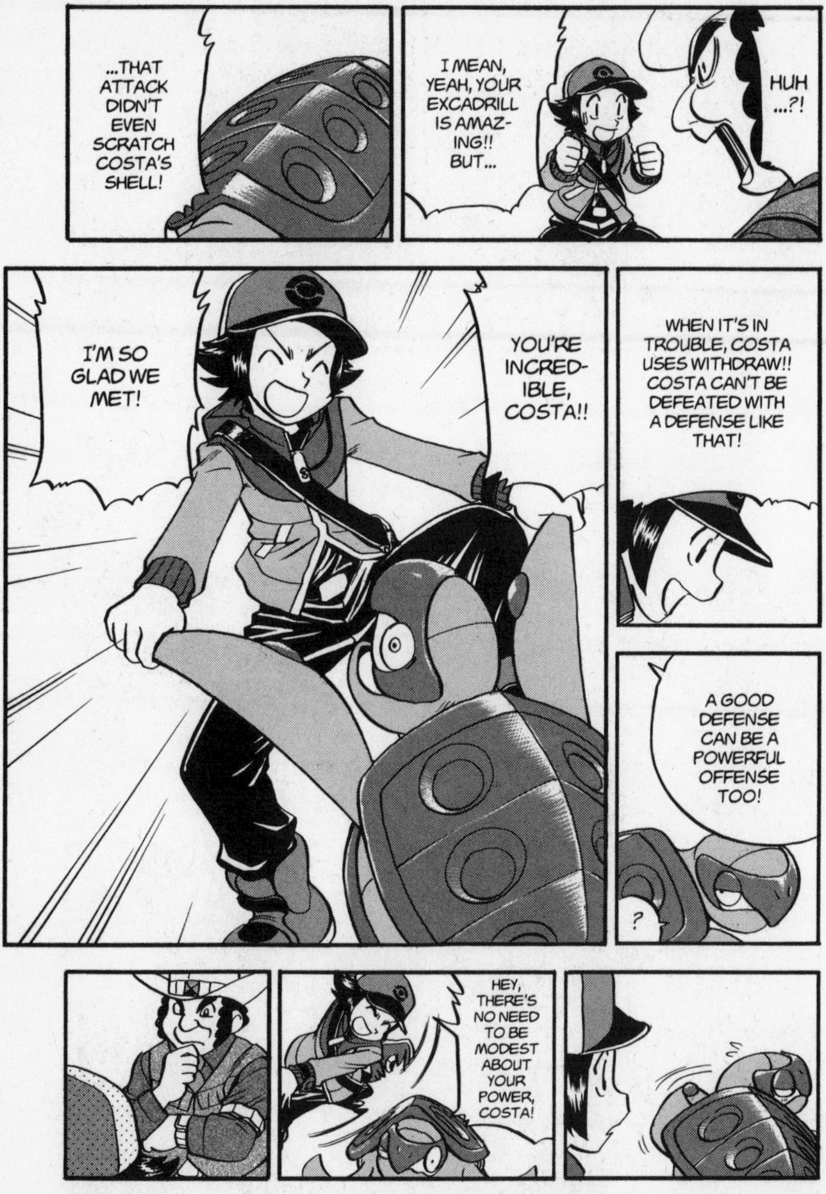
HUH ...?!
I MEAN, YEAH, YOUR EXCADRILL IS AMAZ-ING!! BUT...
...THAT ATTACK DIDN'T EVEN SCRATCH COSTA'S SHELL!
WHEN IT'S IN TROUBLE, COSTA USES WITHDRAW!! COSTA CAN'T BE DEFEATED WITH A DEFENSE LIKE THAT!
A GOOD DEFENSE CAN BE A POWERFUL OFFENSE TOO!
?
YOU'RE INCRED-IBLE, COSTA!!
I'M SO GLAD WE MET!
HEY, THERE'S NO NEED TO BE MODEST ABOUT YOUR POWER, COSTA!

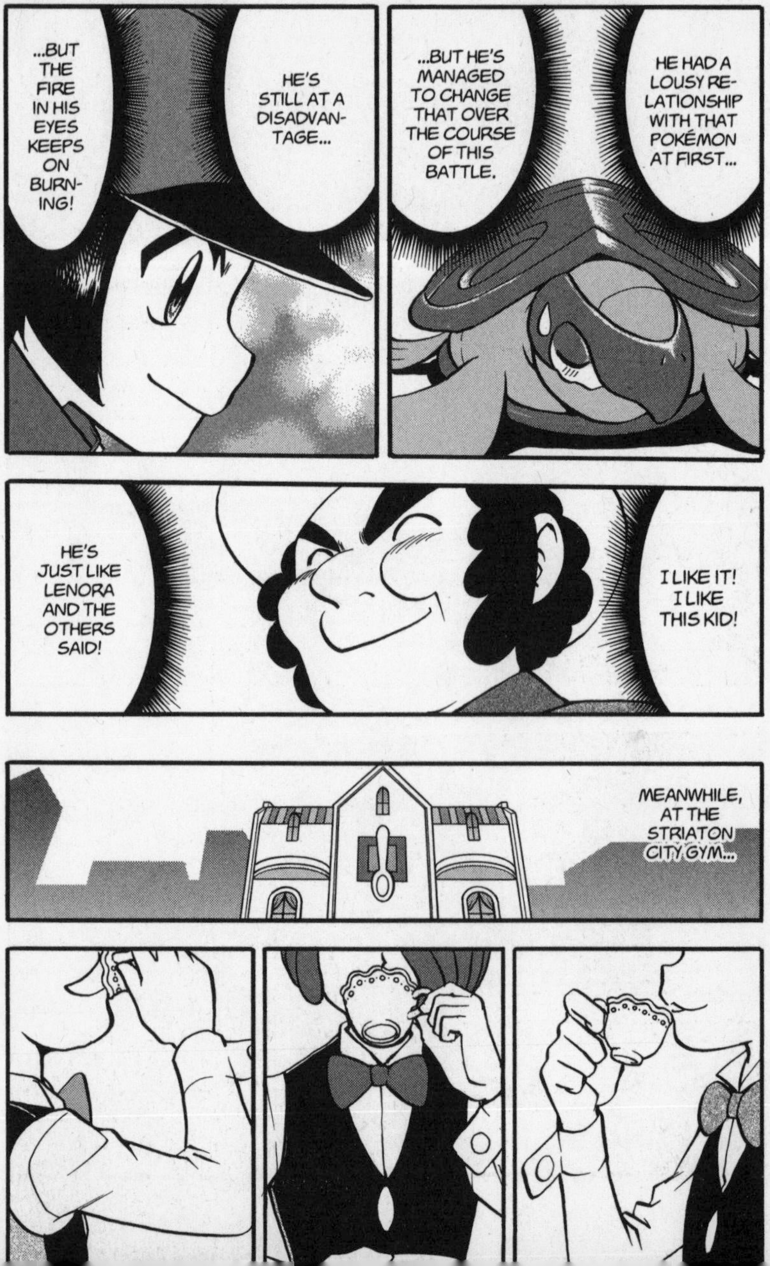
HE HAD A LOUSY RELATIONSHIP WITH THAT POKÉMON AT FIRST...
...BUT HE'S MANAGED TO CHANGE THAT OVER THE COURSE OF THIS BATTLE.
HE'S STILL AT A DISADVANTAGE...
...BUT THE FIRE IN HIS EYES KEEPS ON BURNING!
I LIKE IT! I LIKE THIS KID!
HE'S JUST LIKE LENORA AND THE OTHERS SAID!
MEANWHILE, AT THE STRIATON CITY GYM...

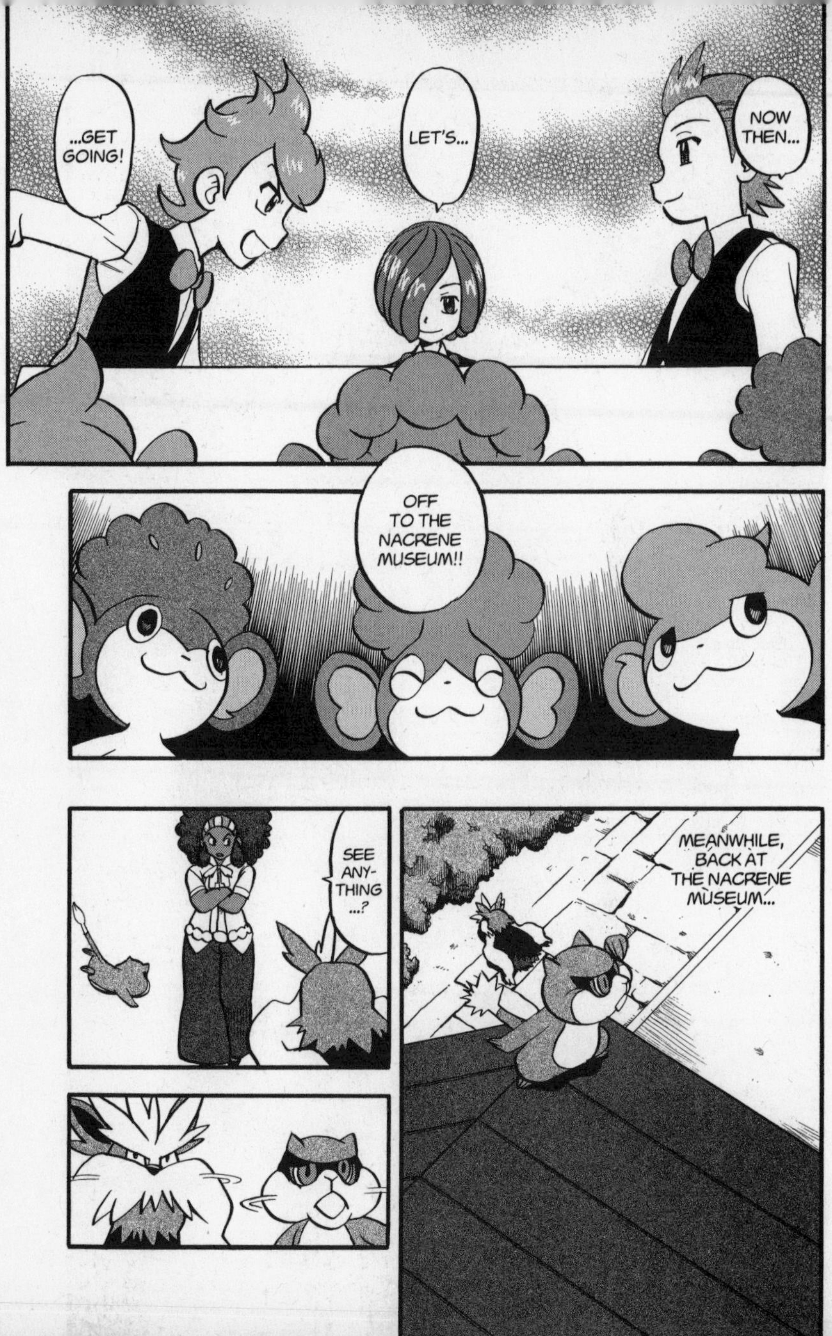
NOW THEN...
LET'S...
...GET GOING!
OFF TO THE NACRENE MUSEUM!!
MEANWHILE, BACK AT THE NACRENE MUSEUM...
SEE ANY-THING ...?

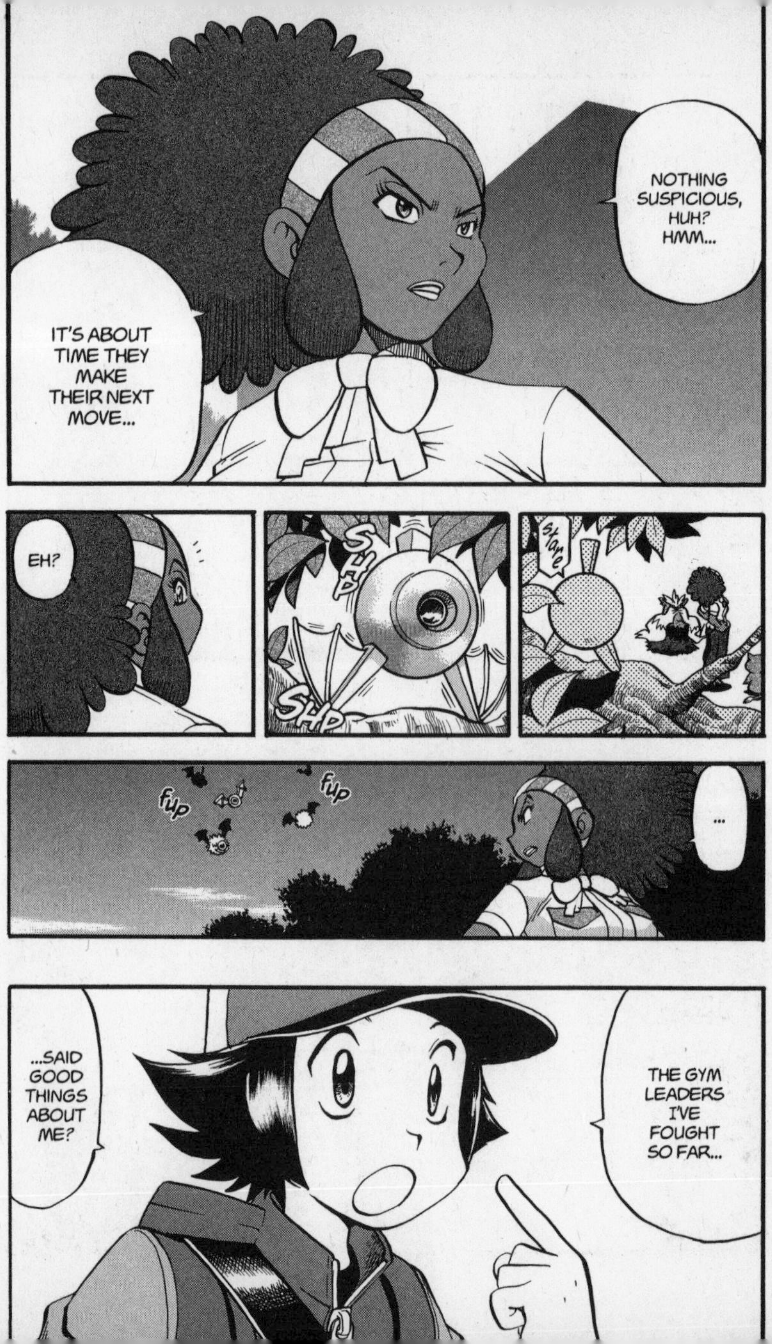
NOTHING SUSPICIOUS, HUH? HMM...
IT'S ABOUT TIME THEY MAKE THEIR NEXT MOVE...
stare
SHP
SHP
EH?
...
fup
fup
THE GYM LEADERS I'VE FOUGHT SO FAR...
...SAID GOOD THINGS ABOUT ME?

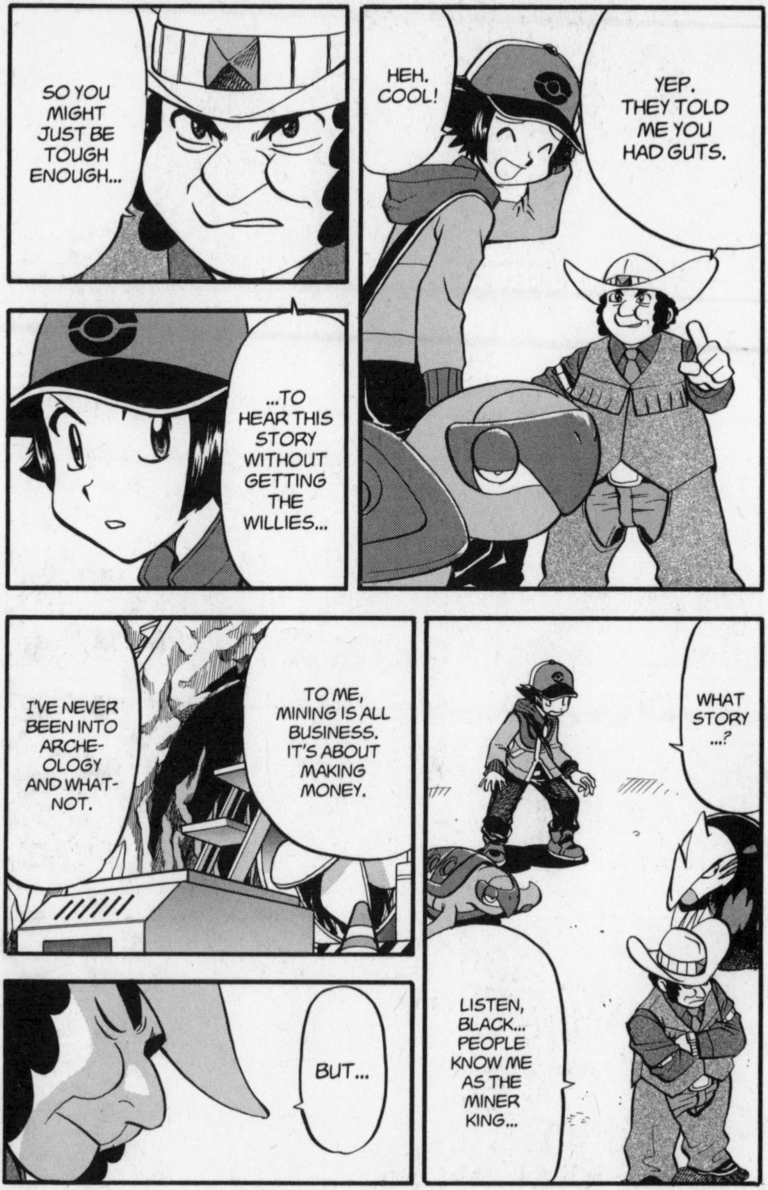
YEP. THEY TOLD ME YOU HAD GUTS.
HEH. COOL!
SO YOU MIGHT JUST BE TOUGH ENOUGH...
...TO HEAR THIS STORY WITHOUT GETTING THE WILLIES...
WHAT STORY ...?
LISTEN, BLACK... PEOPLE KNOW ME AS THE MINER KING...
TO ME, MINING IS ALL BUSINESS. IT'S ABOUT MAKING MONEY.
I'VE NEVER BEEN INTO ARCHE-OLOGY AND WHAT-NOT.
BUT...

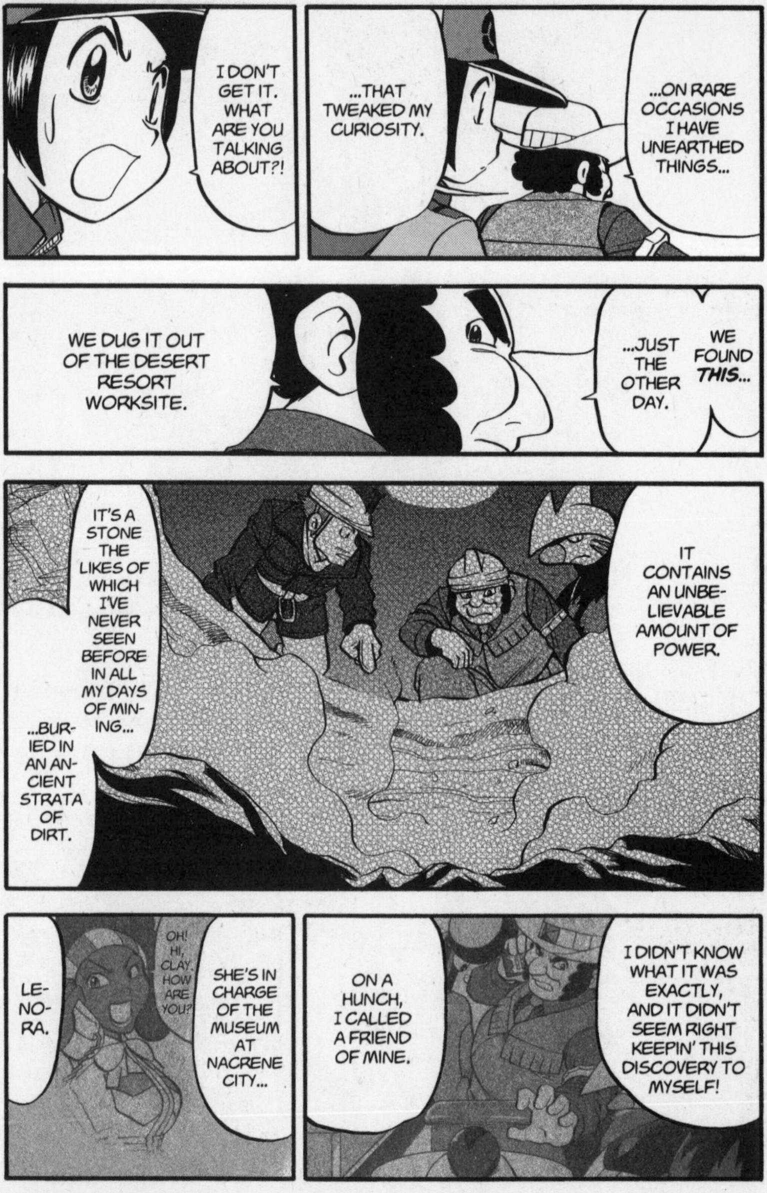
...ON RARE OCCASIONS I HAVE UNEARTHED THINGS...
...THAT TWEAKED MY CURIOSITY.
I DON'T GET IT. WHAT ARE YOU TALKING ABOUT?!
WE FOUND *THIS*...
...JUST THE OTHER DAY.
WE DUG IT OUT OF THE DESERT RESORT WORKSITE.
IT CONTAINS AN UNBE-LIEVABLE AMOUNT OF POWER.
IT'S A STONE THE LIKES OF WHICH I'VE NEVER SEEN BEFORE IN ALL MY DAYS OF MIN-ING...
...BUR-IED IN AN AN-CIENT STRATA OF DIRT.
I DIDN'T KNOW WHAT IT WAS EXACTLY, AND IT DIDN'T SEEM RIGHT KEEPIN' THIS DISCOVERY TO MYSELF!
ON A HUNCH, I CALLED A FRIEND OF MINE.
SHE'S IN CHARGE OF THE MUSEUM AT NACRENE CITY...
OH! HI, CLAY. HOW ARE YOU?
LE-NO-RA.

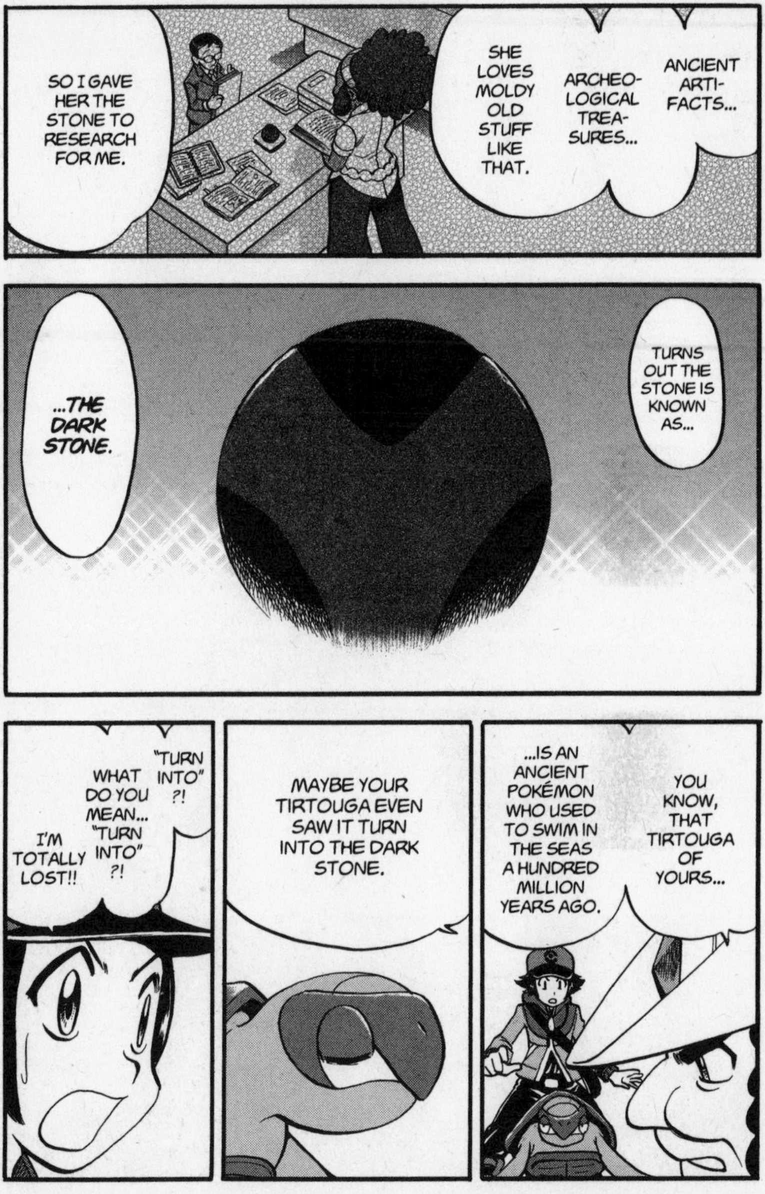
ANCIENT ARTIFACTS...
ARCHEOLOGICAL TREASURES...
SHE LOVES MOLDY OLD STUFF LIKE THAT.
SO I GAVE HER THE STONE TO RESEARCH FOR ME.
TURNS OUT THE STONE IS KNOWN AS...
...THE DARK STONE.
YOU KNOW, THAT TIRTOUGA OF YOURS...
...IS AN ANCIENT POKÉMON WHO USED TO SWIM IN THE SEAS A HUNDRED MILLION YEARS AGO.
MAYBE YOUR TIRTOUGA EVEN SAW IT TURN INTO THE DARK STONE.
"TURN INTO" ?!
WHAT DO YOU MEAN... "TURN INTO" ?!
I'M TOTALLY LOST!!

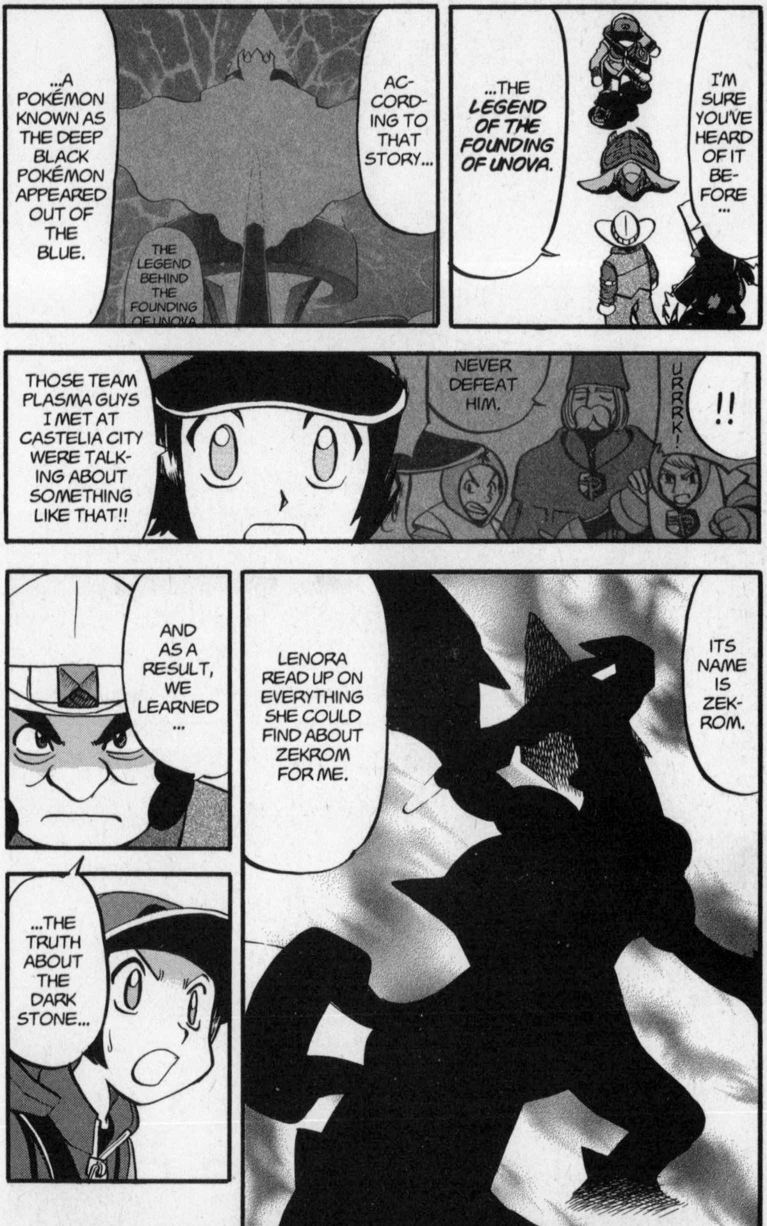
I'M SURE YOU'VE HEARD OF IT BEFORE...
...THE LEGEND OF THE FOUNDING OF UNOVA.
ACCORDING TO THAT STORY...
...A POKÉMON KNOWN AS THE DEEP BLACK POKÉMON APPEARED OUT OF THE BLUE.
THE LEGEND BEHIND THE FOUNDING OF UNOVA
!!
URRRK!
NEVER DEFEAT HIM.
THOSE TEAM PLASMA GUYS I MET AT CASTELIA CITY WERE TALKING ABOUT SOMETHING LIKE THAT!!
ITS NAME IS ZEKROM.
LENORA READ UP ON EVERYTHING SHE COULD FIND ABOUT ZEKROM FOR ME.
AND AS A RESULT, WE LEARNED...
...THE TRUTH ABOUT THE DARK STONE...

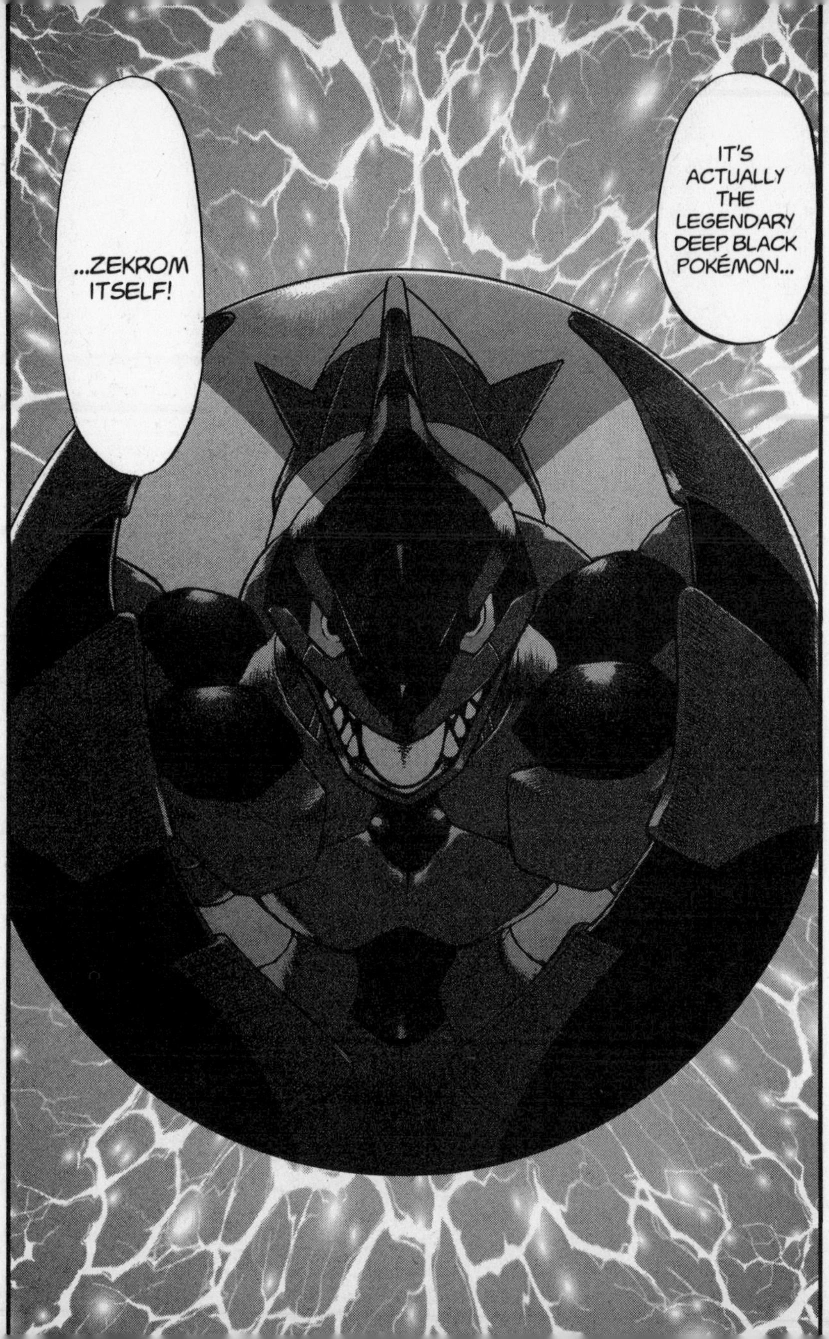
IT'S ACTUALLY THE LEGENDARY DEEP BLACK POKÉMON...
...ZEKROM ITSELF!

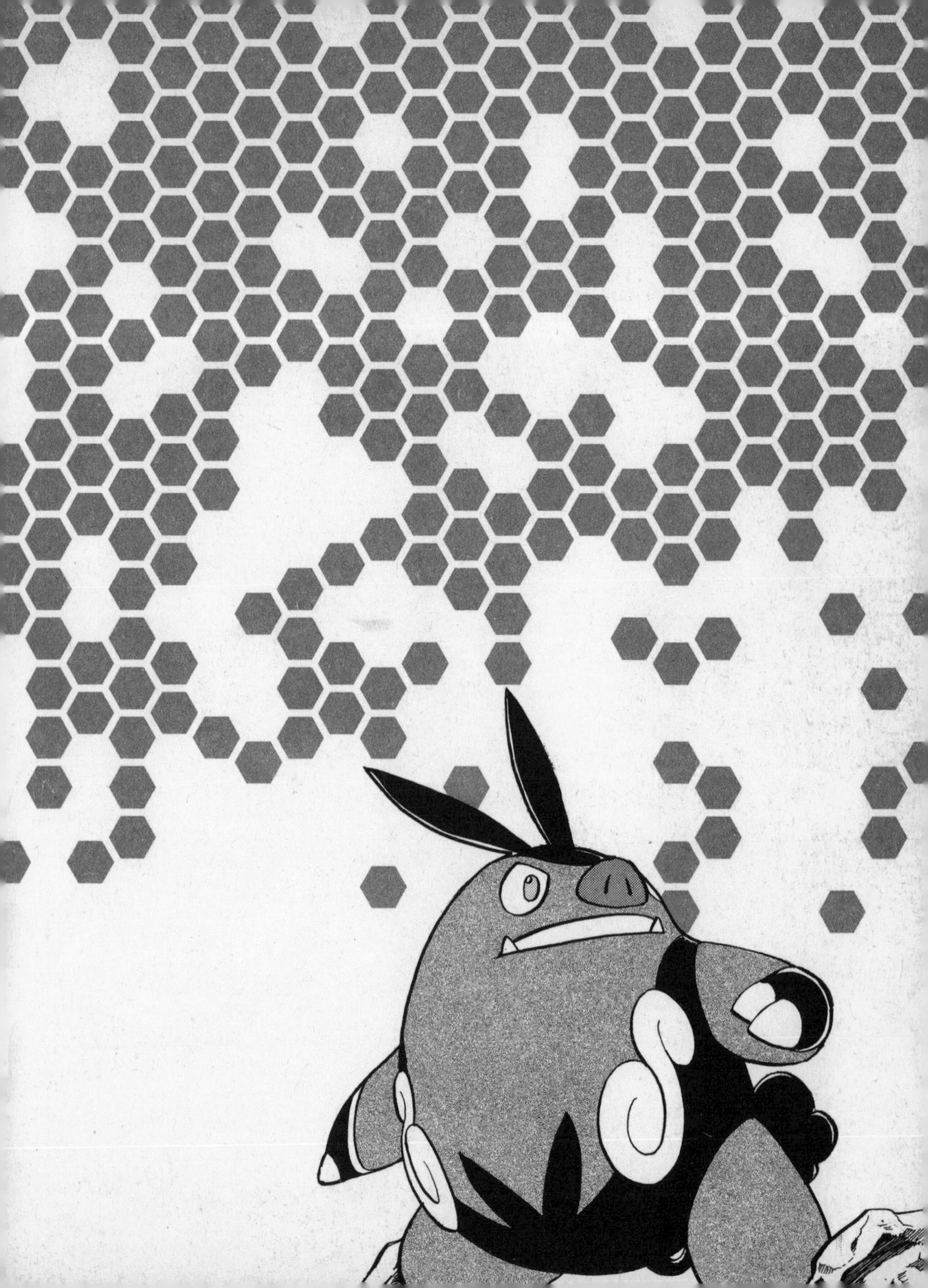

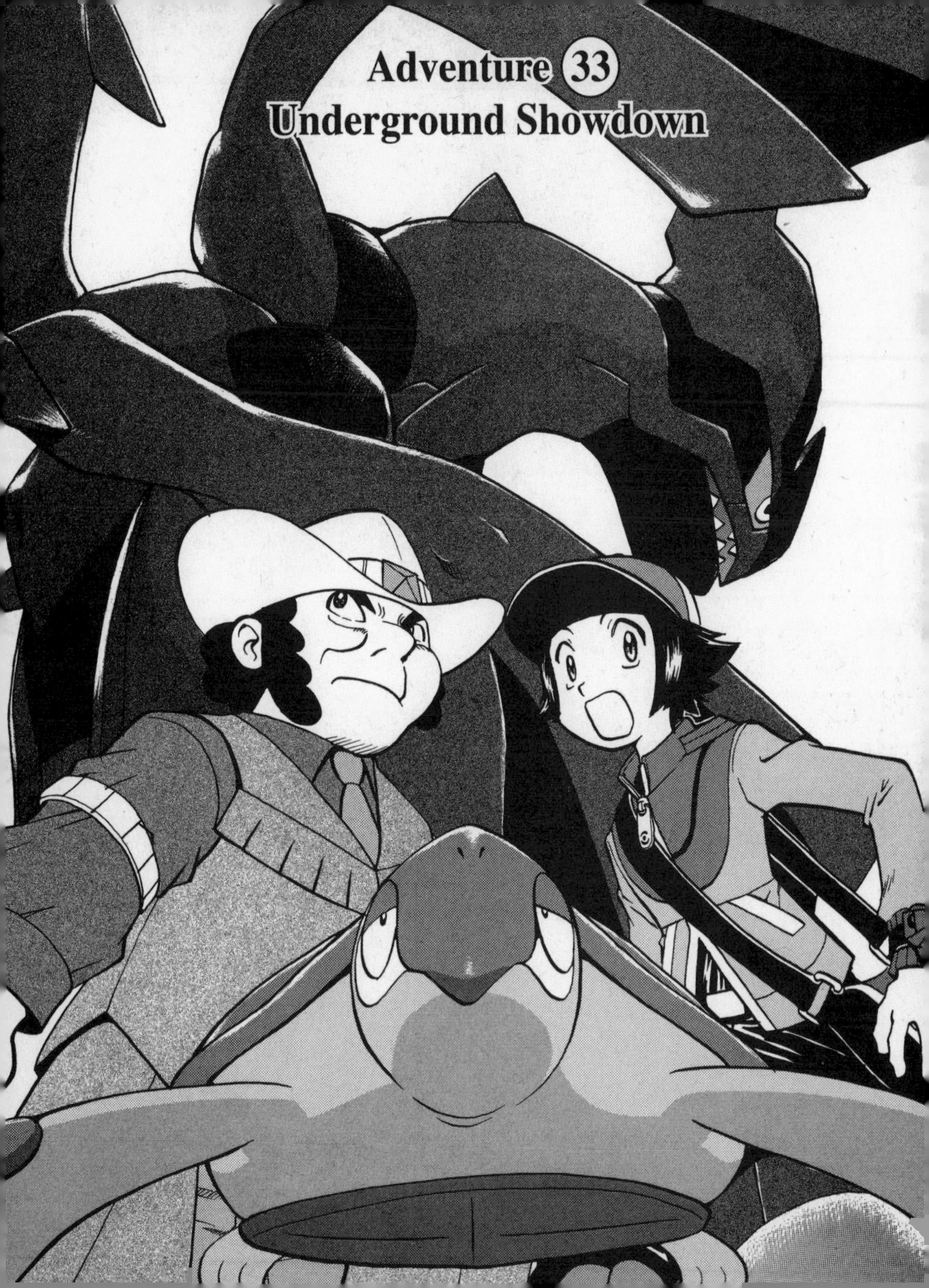
Adventure 33
Underground Showdown

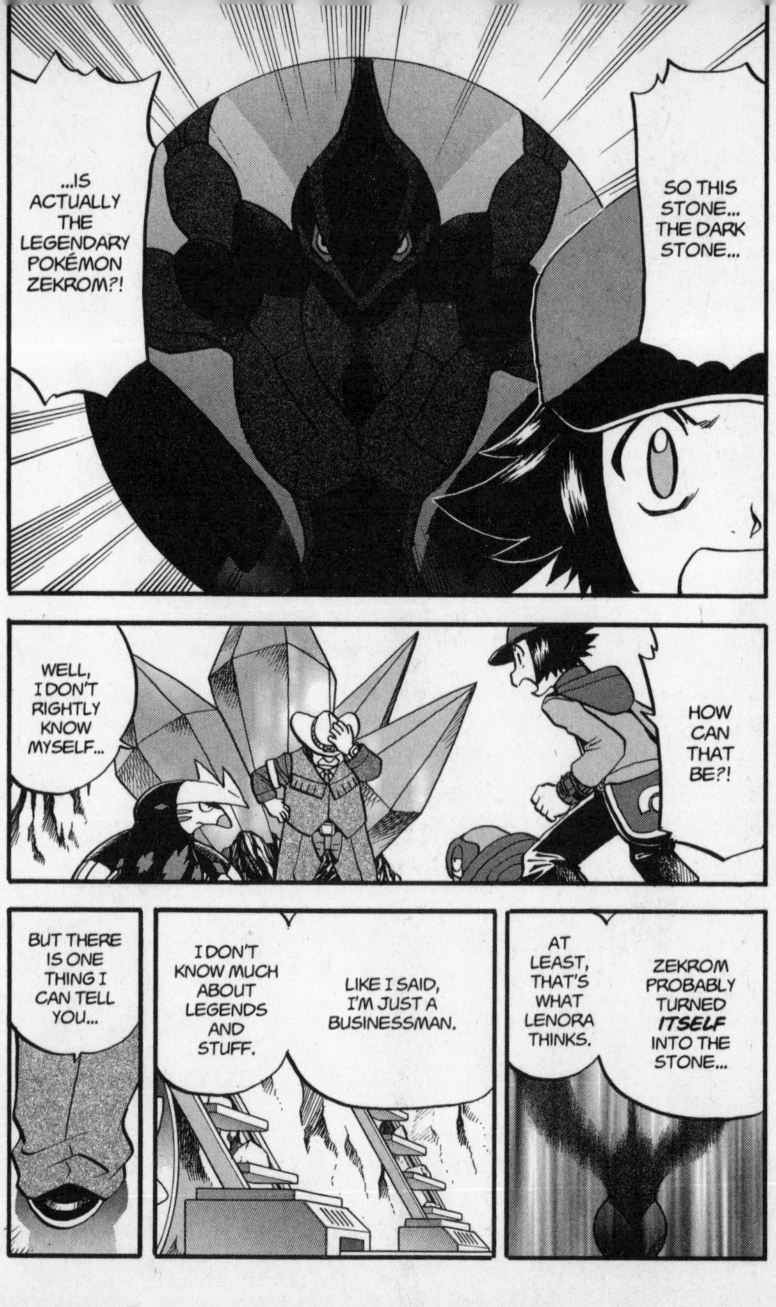
SO THIS STONE... THE DARK STONE...
...IS ACTUALLY THE LEGENDARY POKÉMON ZEKROM?!
HOW CAN THAT BE?!
WELL, I DON'T RIGHTLY KNOW MYSELF...
ZEKROM PROBABLY TURNED *ITSELF* INTO THE STONE...
AT LEAST, THAT'S WHAT LENORA THINKS.
LIKE I SAID, I'M JUST A BUSINESSMAN.
I DON'T KNOW MUCH ABOUT LEGENDS AND STUFF.
BUT THERE IS ONE THING I CAN TELL YOU...

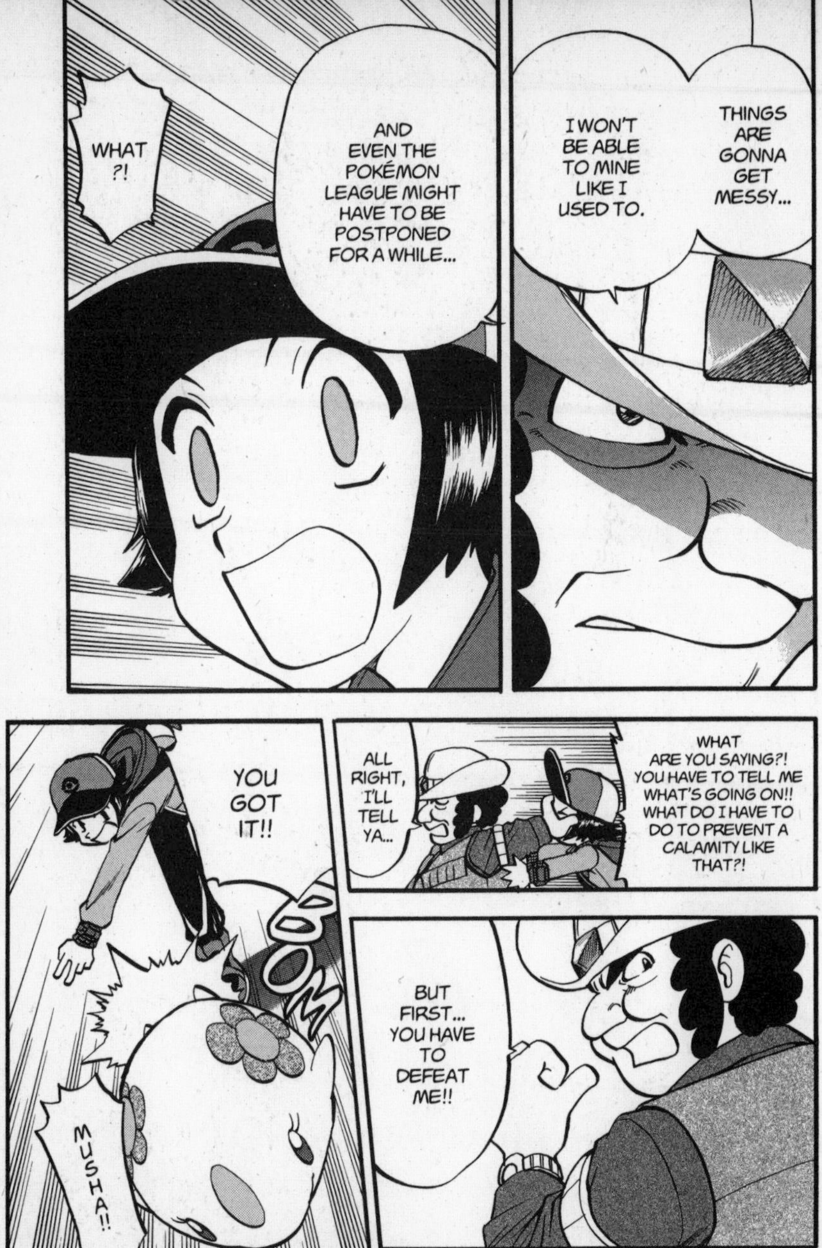
THINGS ARE GONNA GET MESSY...
I WON'T BE ABLE TO MINE LIKE I USED TO.
AND EVEN THE POKÉMON LEAGUE MIGHT HAVE TO BE POSTPONED FOR A WHILE...
WHAT?!
WHAT ARE YOU SAYING?! YOU HAVE TO TELL ME WHAT'S GOING ON!! WHAT DO I HAVE TO DO TO PREVENT A CALAMITY LIKE THAT?!
ALL RIGHT, I'LL TELL YA...
BUT FIRST... YOU HAVE TO DEFEAT ME!!
YOU GOT IT!!
BOOM
MUSHA!!

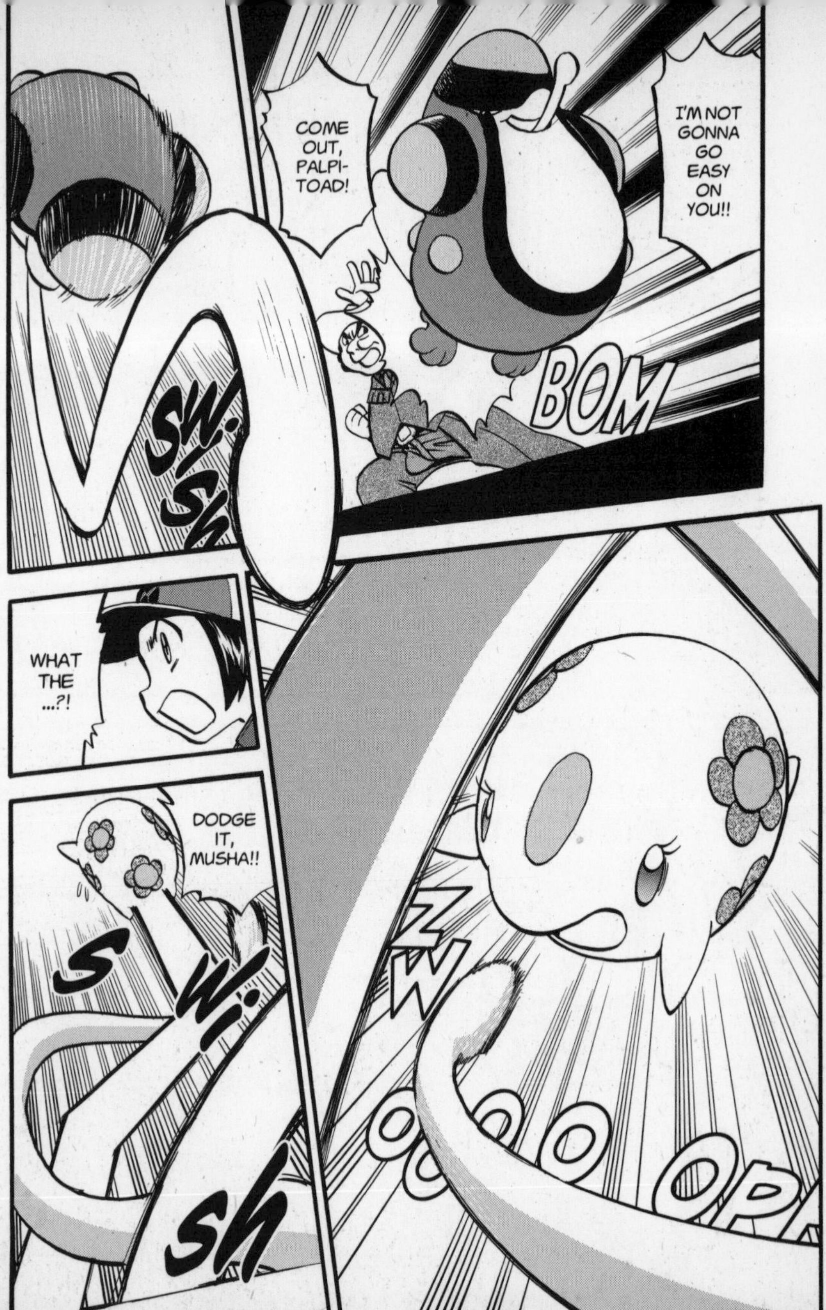
I'M NOT GONNA GO EASY ON YOU!!
COME OUT, PALPITOAD!
BOM
SWISH
ZWOOOOOOOP
WHAT THE ...?!
DODGE IT, MUSHA!!
SWISH

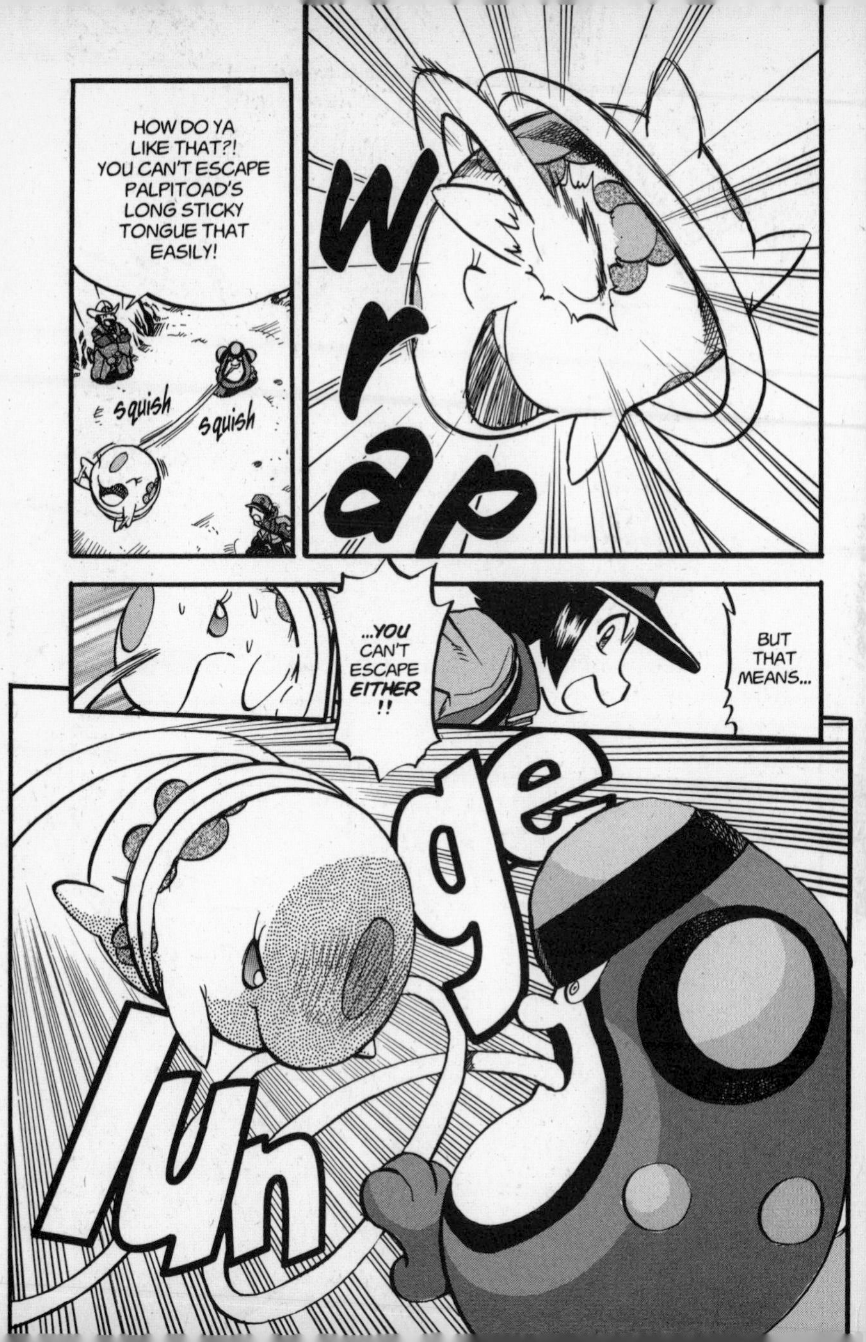
wrap
HOW DO YA LIKE THAT?! YOU CAN'T ESCAPE PALPITOAD'S LONG STICKY TONGUE THAT EASILY!
squish
squish
BUT THAT MEANS...
...YOU CAN'T ESCAPE EITHER!!
lunge

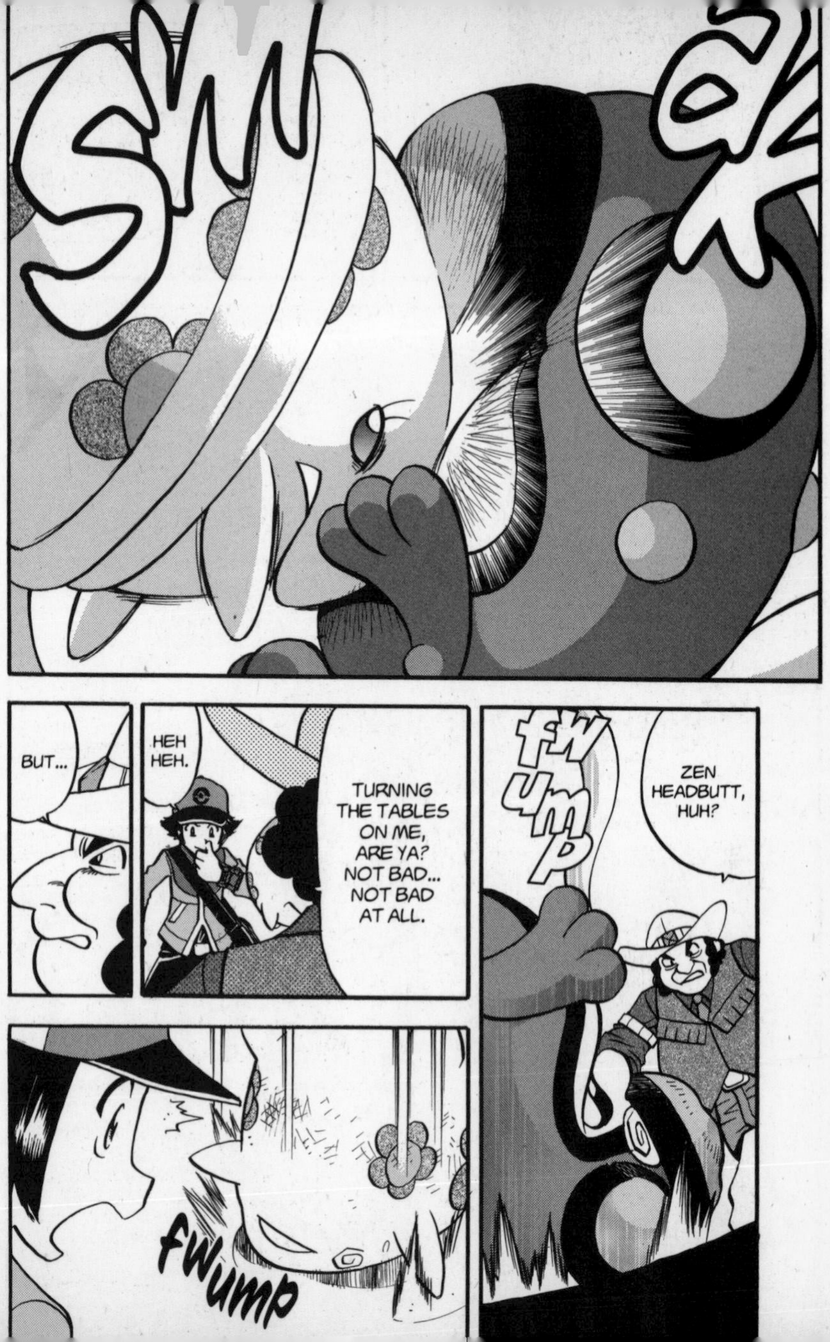
ZEN HEADBUTT, HUH?
FWUMP
TURNING THE TABLES ON ME, ARE YA? NOT BAD... NOT BAD AT ALL.
HEH HEH.
BUT...
FWUMP

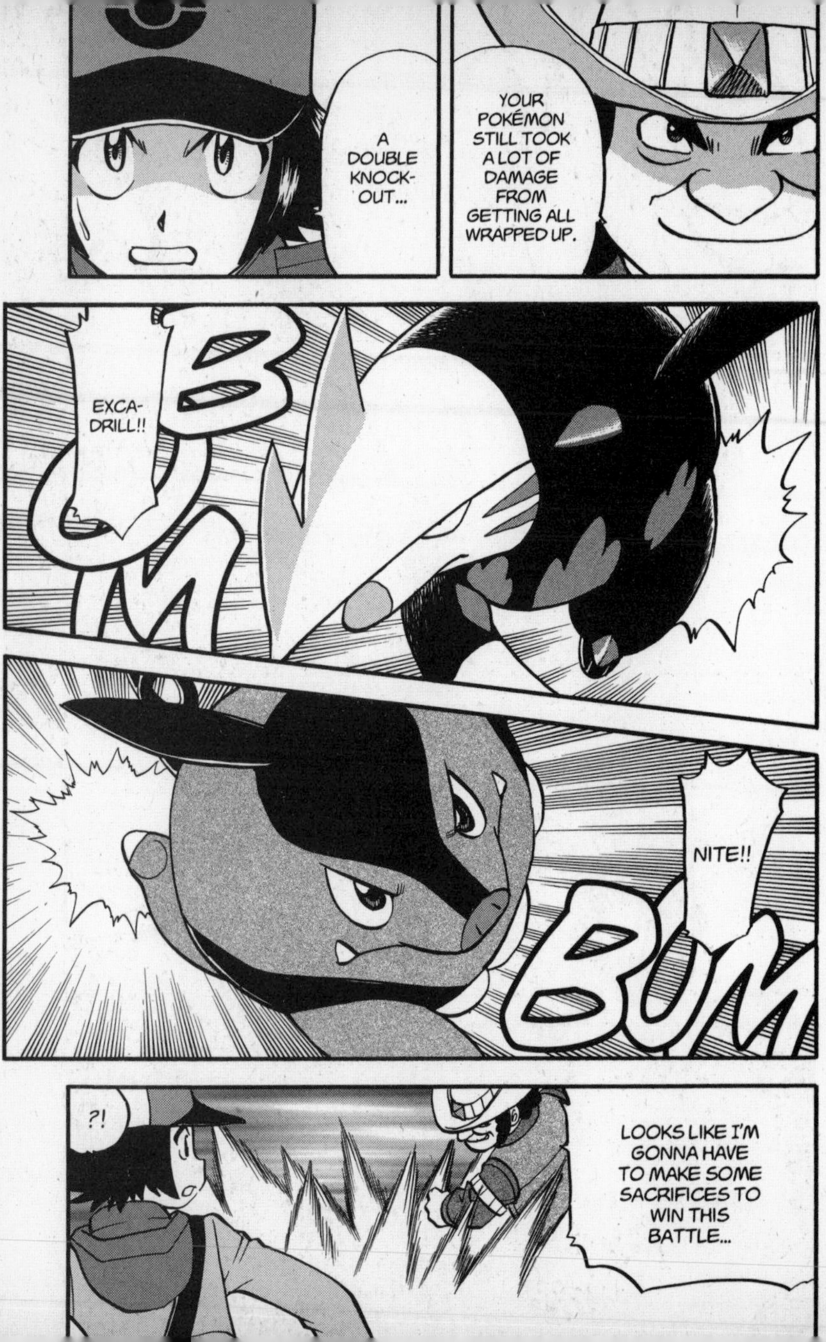
YOUR POKÉMON STILL TOOK A LOT OF DAMAGE FROM GETTING ALL WRAPPED UP.
A DOUBLE KNOCK-OUT...
BUM
EXCA-DRILL!!
NITE!!
BUM
LOOKS LIKE I'M GONNA HAVE TO MAKE SOME SACRIFICES TO WIN THIS BATTLE...
?!

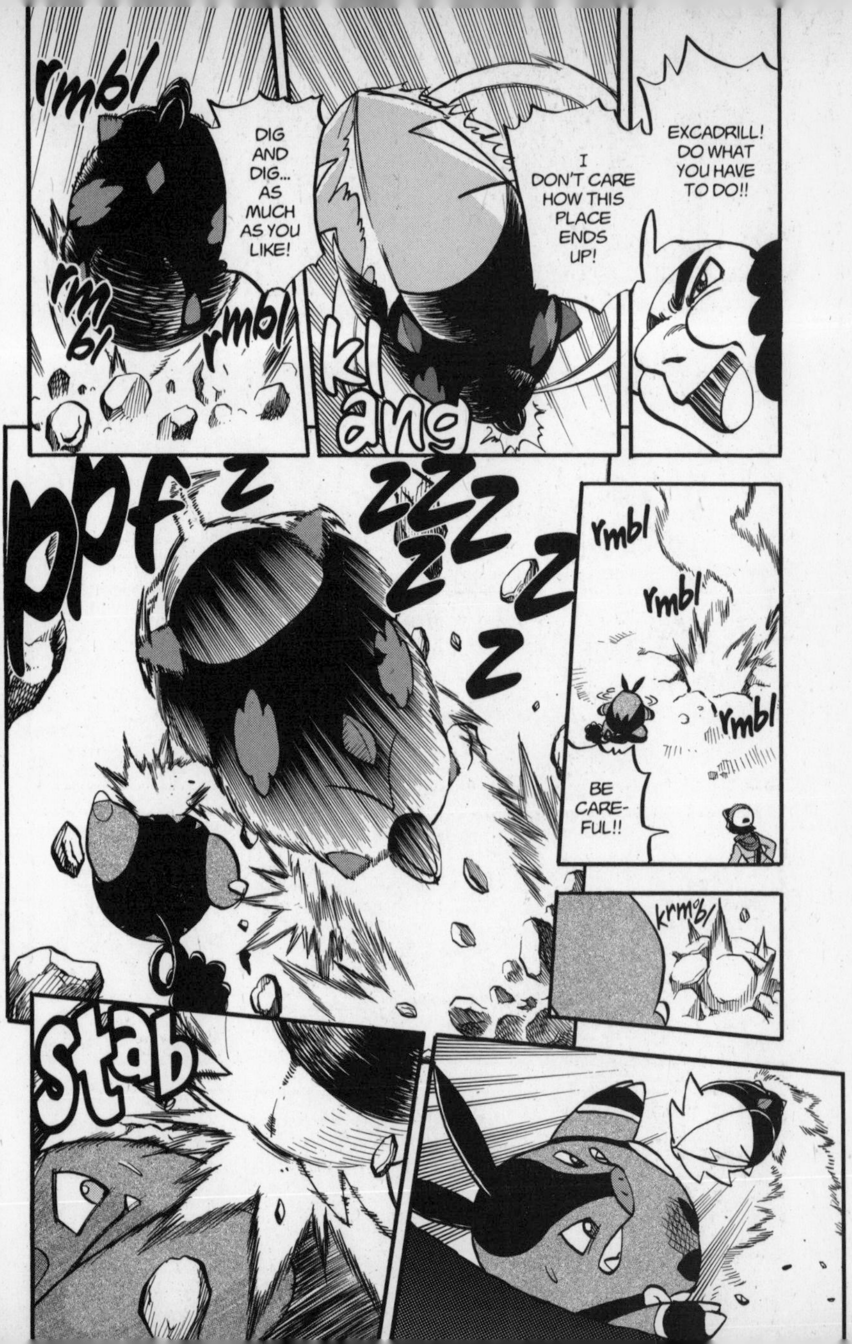
EXCADRILL! DO WHAT YOU HAVE TO DO!!
I DON'T CARE HOW THIS PLACE ENDS UP!
kl ang
rmbl
DIG AND DIG... AS MUCH AS YOU LIKE!
rmbl
rmbl
rmbl
rmbl
rmbl
BE CAREFUL!!
krmbl
ppf
z
zzzz
z
z
stab

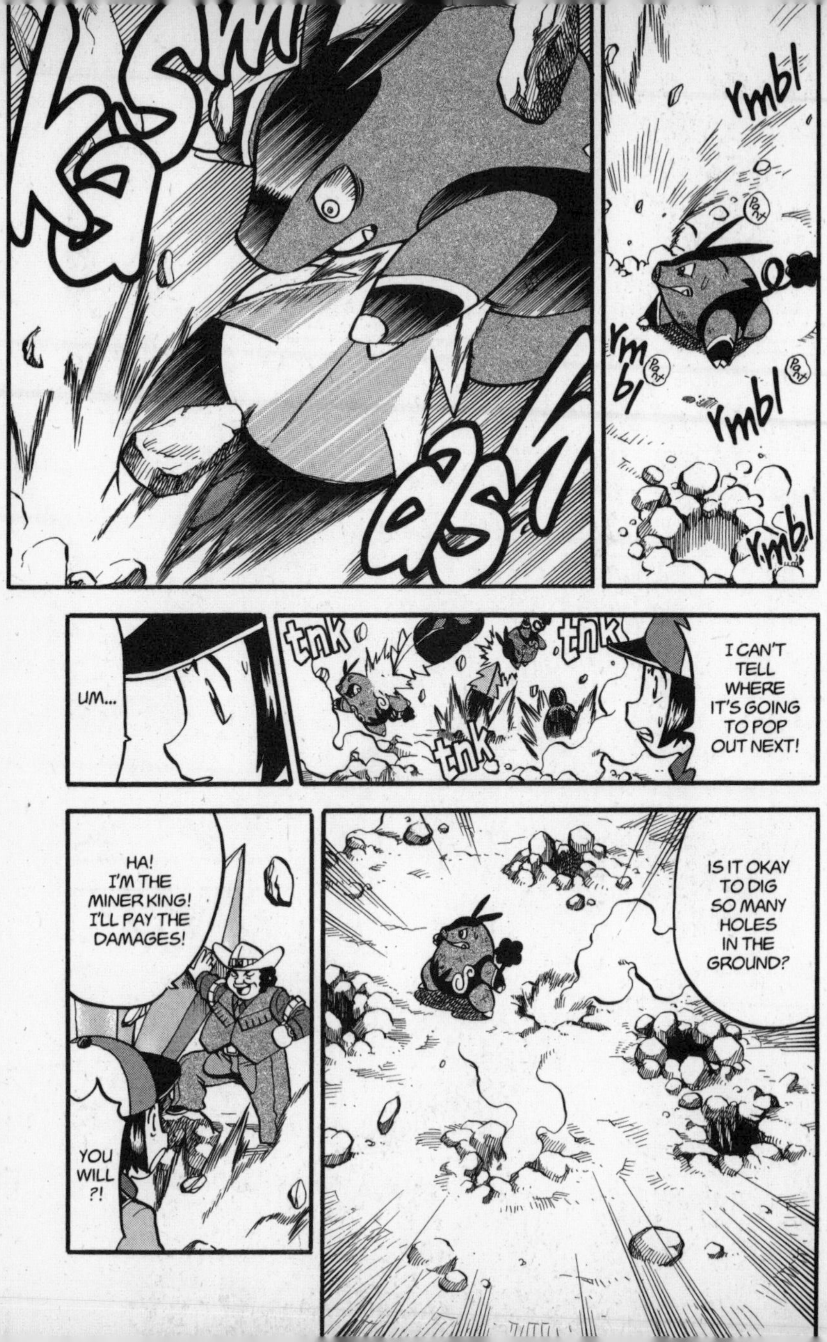
Rmbl
Pant
Rmbl
Pant
Rmbl
Rmbl
I CAN'T TELL WHERE IT'S GOING TO POP OUT NEXT!
tnk
tnk
tnk
UM...
IS IT OKAY TO DIG SO MANY HOLES IN THE GROUND?
HA! I'M THE MINER KING! I'LL PAY THE DAMAGES!
YOU WILL?!

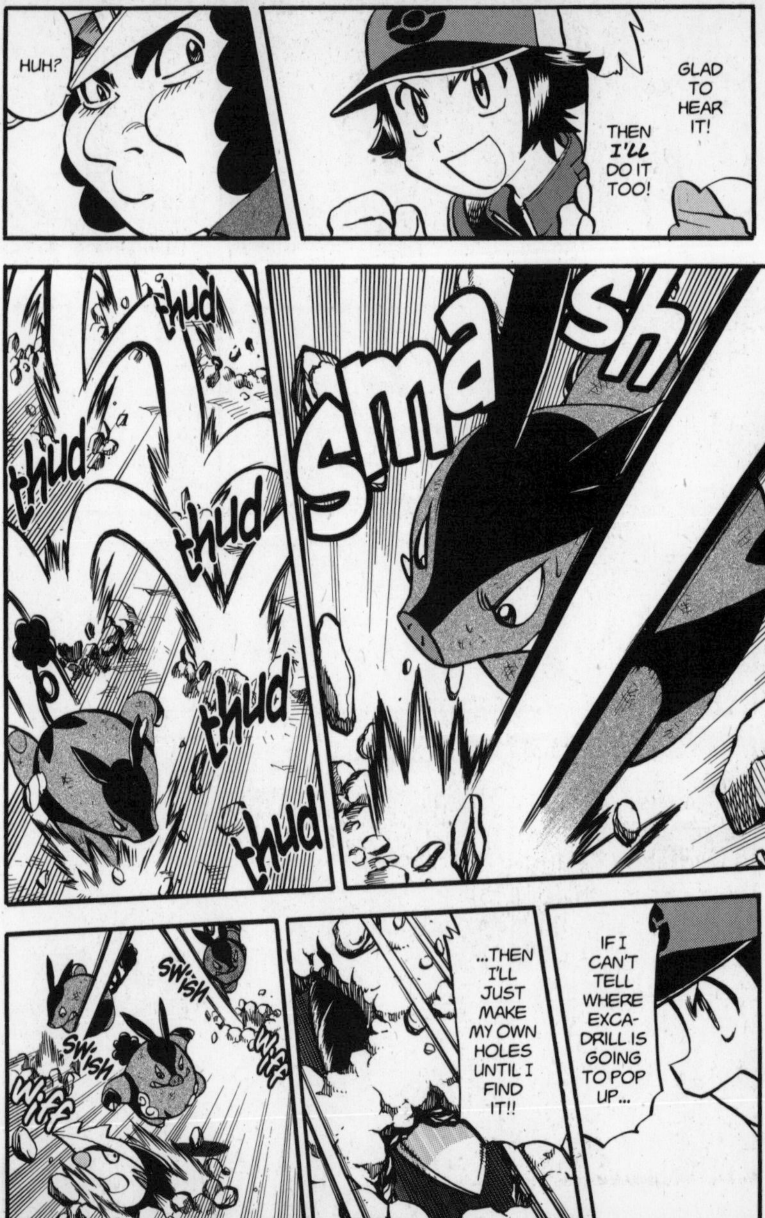
GLAD TO HEAR IT!
THEN I'LL DO IT TOO!
HUH?
smash
thud
thud
thud
thud
thud
IF I CAN'T TELL WHERE EXCA-DRILL IS GOING TO POP UP...
...THEN I'LL JUST MAKE MY OWN HOLES UNTIL I FIND IT!!
SWISH
SWISH
WIFF
WIFF

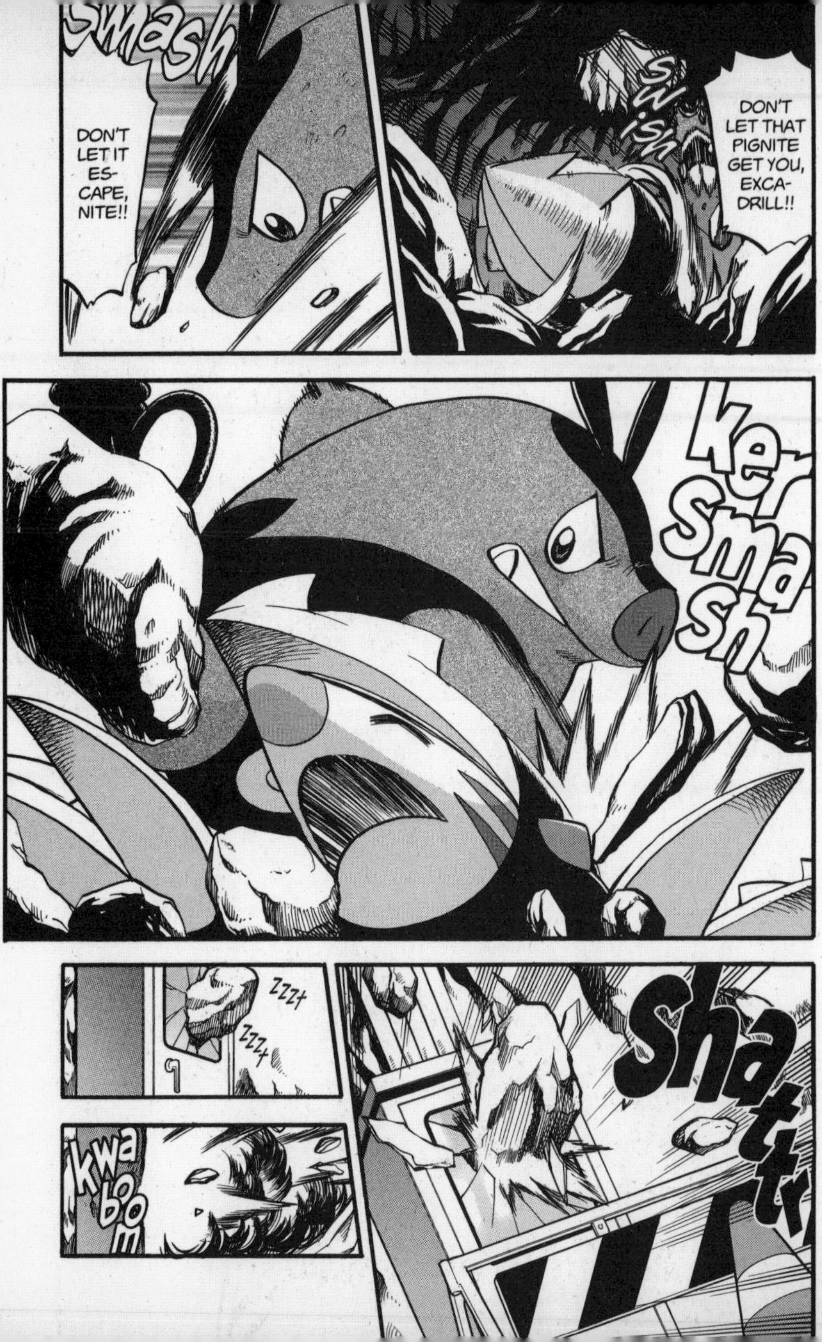
swish
DON'T LET THAT PIGNITE GET YOU, EXCADRILL!!
smash
DON'T LET IT ESCAPE, NITE!!
ker-smash
shattr
zzzt
zzzt
kwaboom

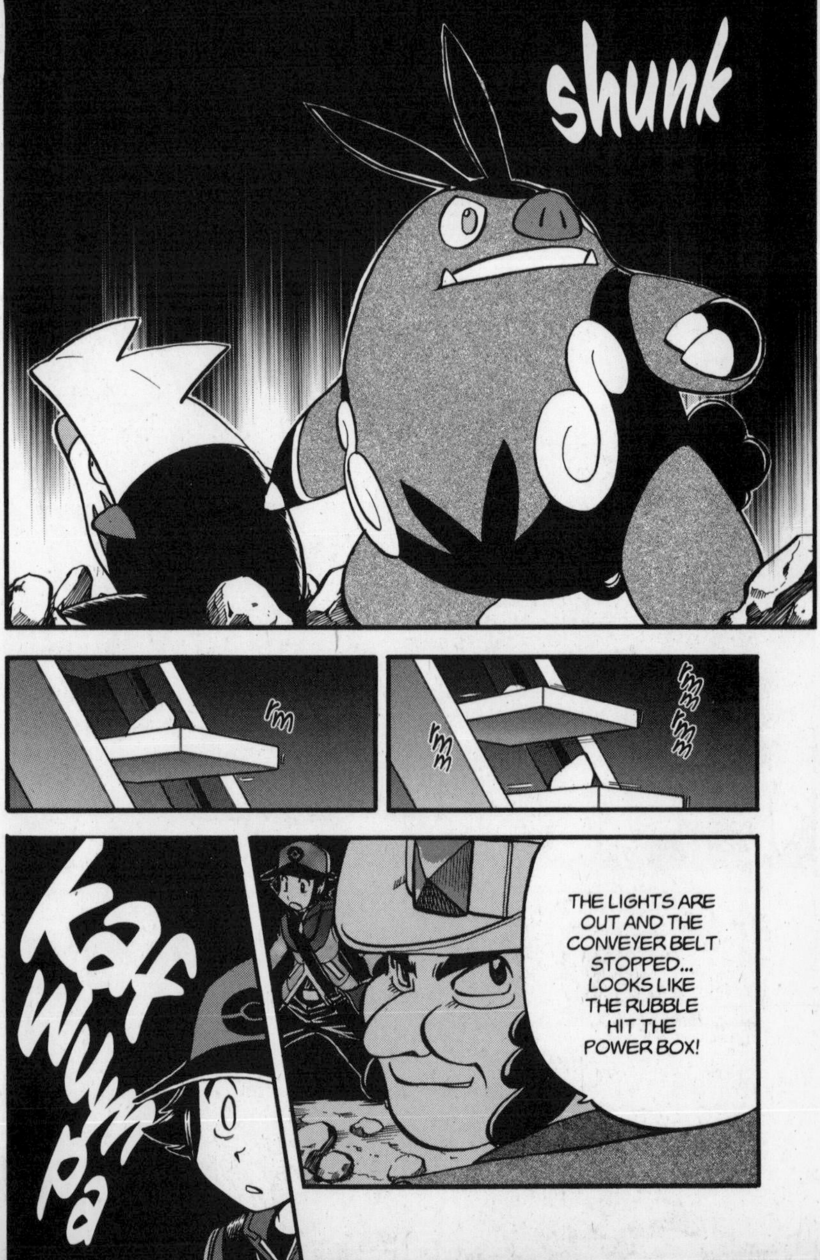
shunk
rmm rmm
rmm
rm
THE LIGHTS ARE OUT AND THE CONVEYER BELT STOPPED... LOOKS LIKE THE RUBBLE HIT THE POWER BOX!
kaf wum pa

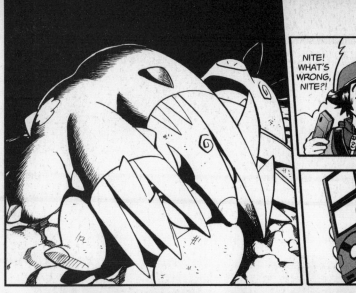

NITE! WHAT'S WRONG, NITE?!

WHAT ...?!

THAT MEANS ...

AN-OTHER DOUBLE KNOCK-OUT!

...JUST ONE POKÉ-MON LEFT.

BOM

WE BOTH HAVE...

BOM

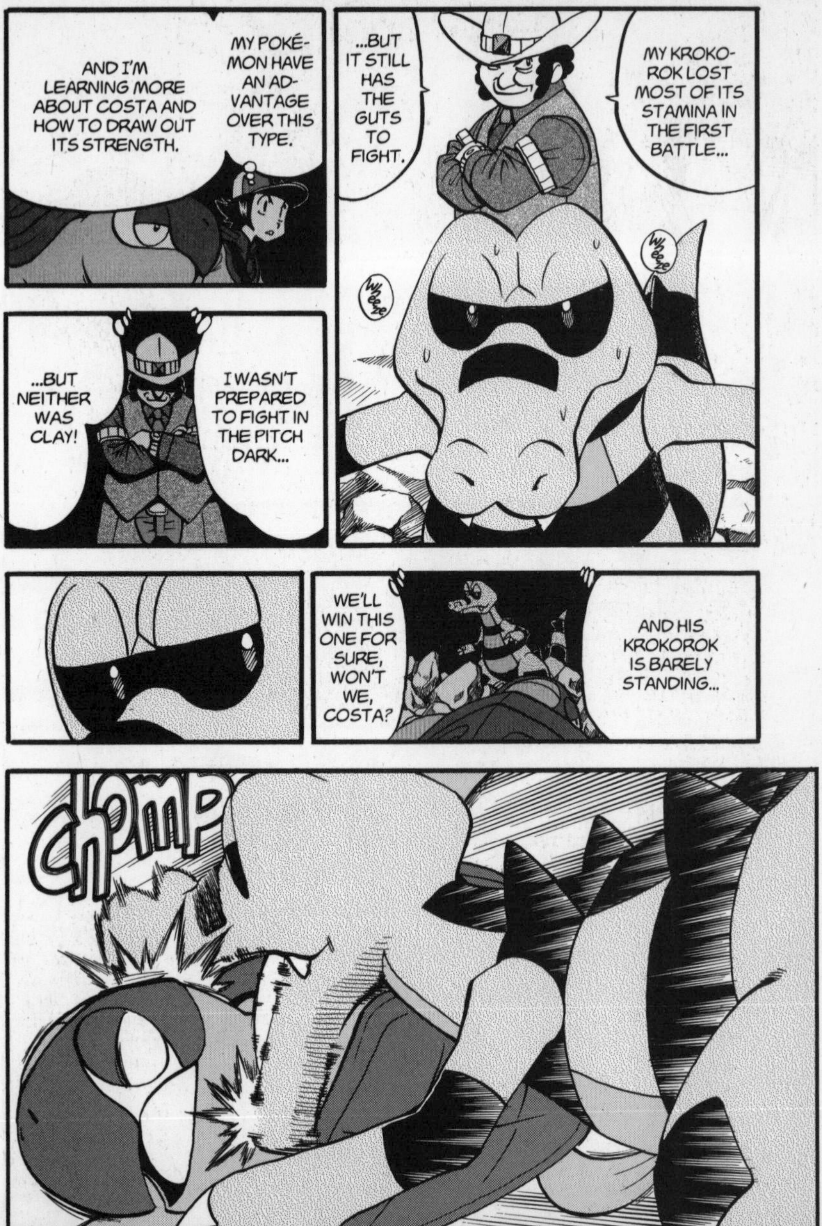
MY KROKOROK LOST MOST OF ITS STAMINA IN THE FIRST BATTLE...
...BUT IT STILL HAS THE GUTS TO FIGHT.
wheeze
wheeze
MY POKÉMON HAVE AN ADVANTAGE OVER THIS TYPE.
AND I'M LEARNING MORE ABOUT COSTA AND HOW TO DRAW OUT ITS STRENGTH.
I WASN'T PREPARED TO FIGHT IN THE PITCH DARK...
...BUT NEITHER WAS CLAY!
AND HIS KROKOROK IS BARELY STANDING...
WE'LL WIN THIS ONE FOR SURE, WON'T WE, COSTA?
CHOMP

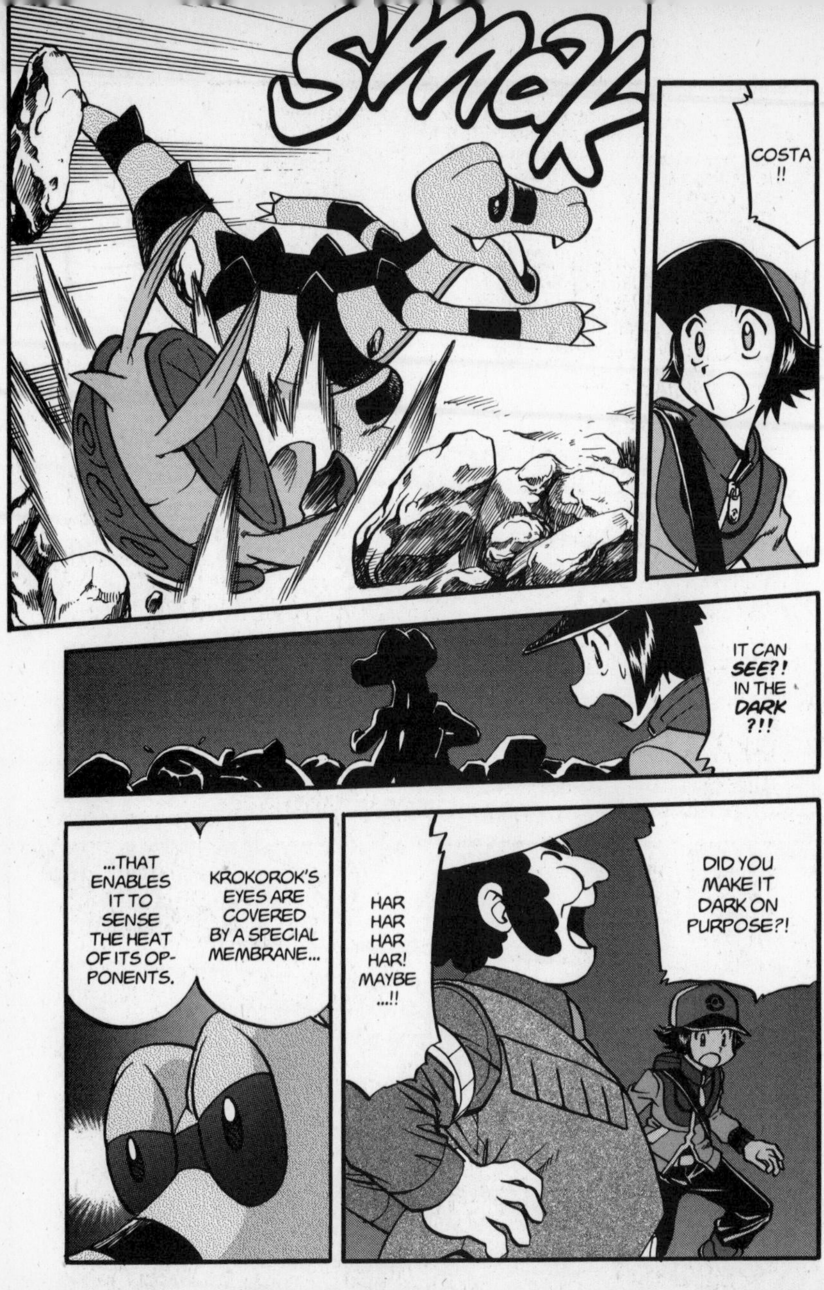
COSTA !!
SMAK
IT CAN SEE?! IN THE DARK ?!!
DID YOU MAKE IT DARK ON PURPOSE?!
HAR HAR HAR HAR! MAYBE ...!!
KROKOROK'S EYES ARE COVERED BY A SPECIAL MEMBRANE...
...THAT ENABLES IT TO SENSE THE HEAT OF ITS OP-PONENTS.

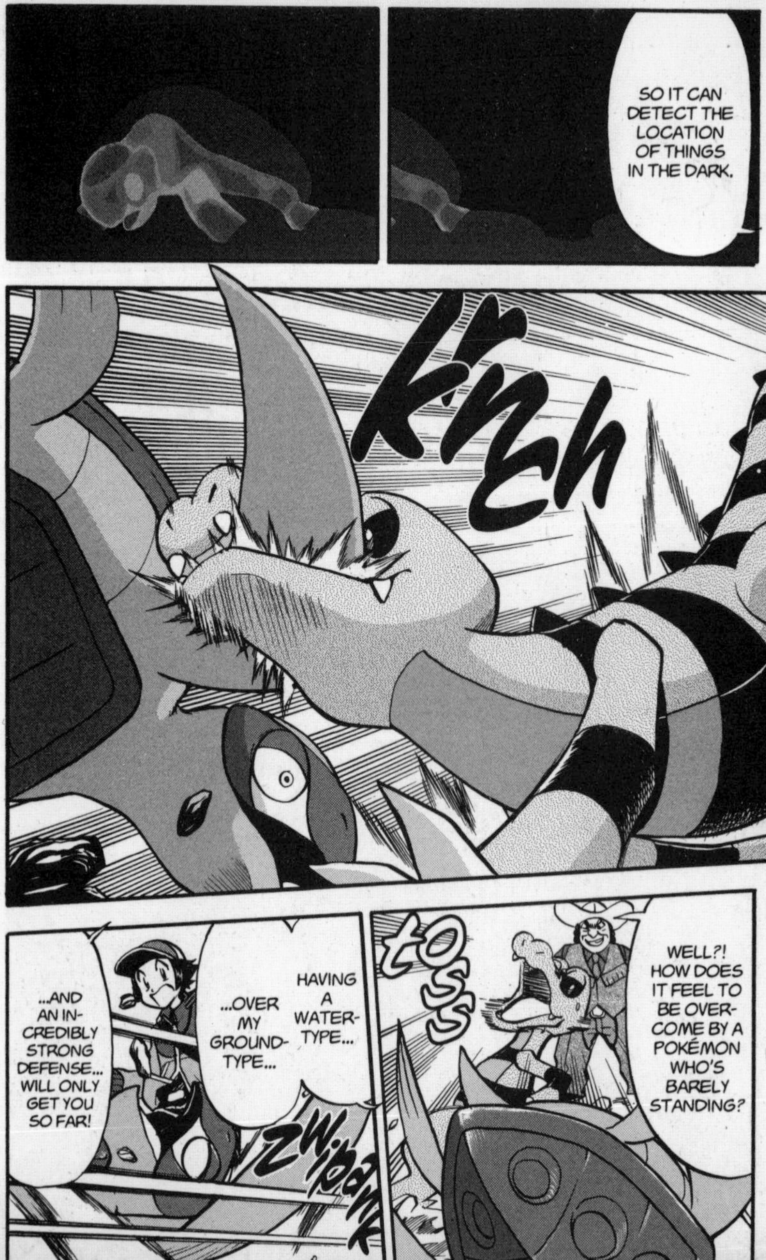
SO IT CAN DETECT THE LOCATION OF THINGS IN THE DARK.
krnch
toss
WELL?! HOW DOES IT FEEL TO BE OVER-COME BY A POKÉMON WHO'S BARELY STANDING?
HAVING A WATER-TYPE...
...OVER MY GROUND-TYPE...
...AND AN IN-CREDIBLY STRONG DEFENSE... WILL ONLY GET YOU SO FAR!
zwipank

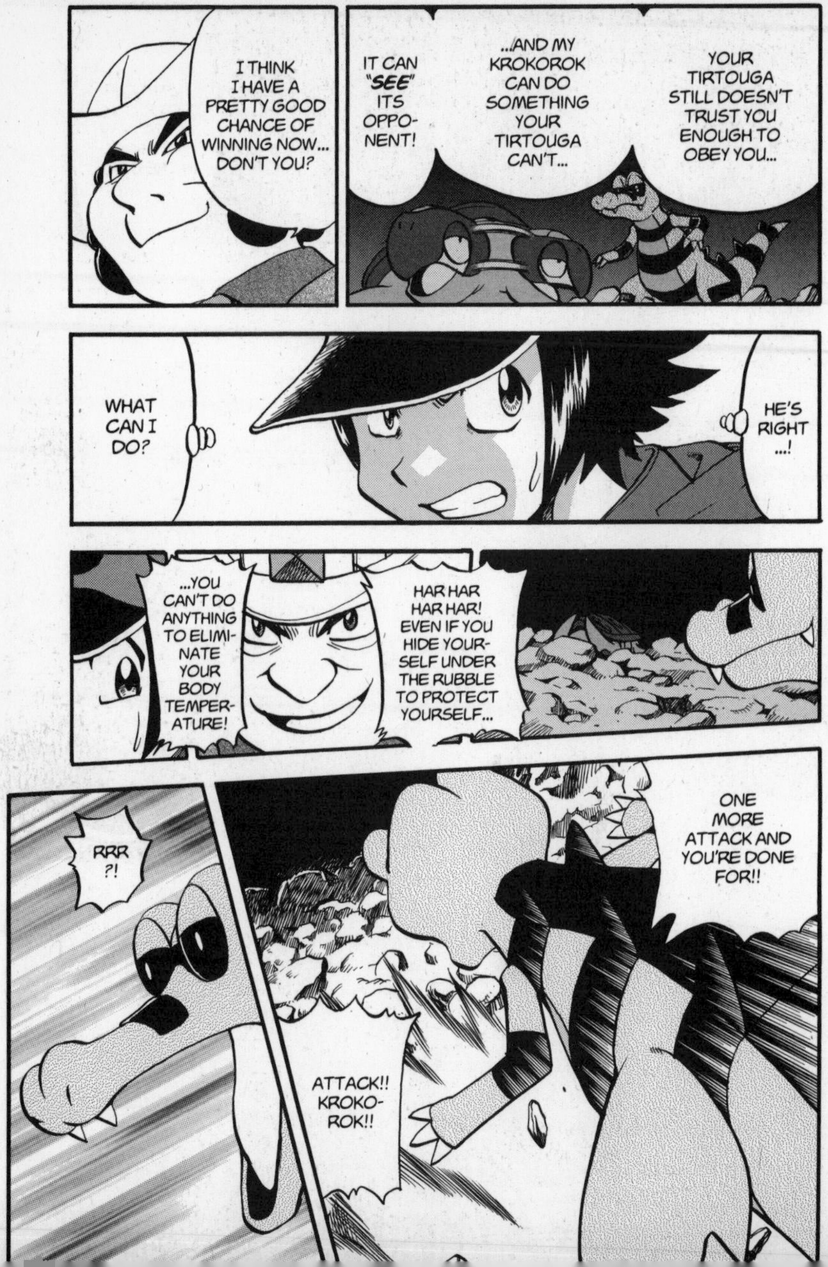
YOUR TIRTOUGA STILL DOESN'T TRUST YOU ENOUGH TO OBEY YOU...
...AND MY KROKOROK CAN DO SOMETHING YOUR TIRTOUGA CAN'T...
IT CAN "SEE" ITS OPPONENT!
I THINK I HAVE A PRETTY GOOD CHANCE OF WINNING NOW... DON'T YOU?
HE'S RIGHT ...!
WHAT CAN I DO?
HAR HAR HAR! EVEN IF YOU HIDE YOURSELF UNDER THE RUBBLE TO PROTECT YOURSELF...
...YOU CAN'T DO ANYTHING TO ELIMINATE YOUR BODY TEMPERATURE!
ONE MORE ATTACK AND YOU'RE DONE FOR!!
ATTACK!! KROKOROK!!
RRR ?!

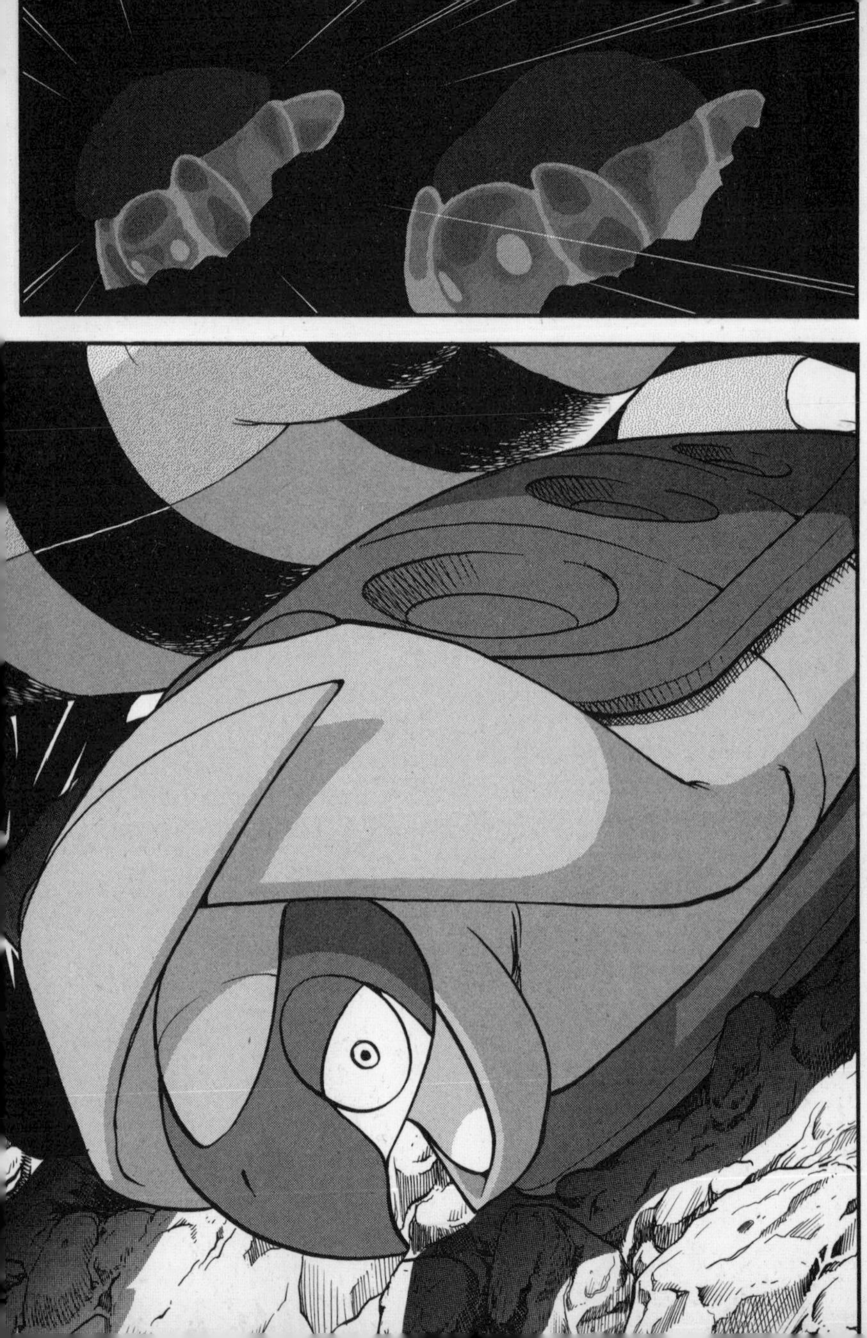

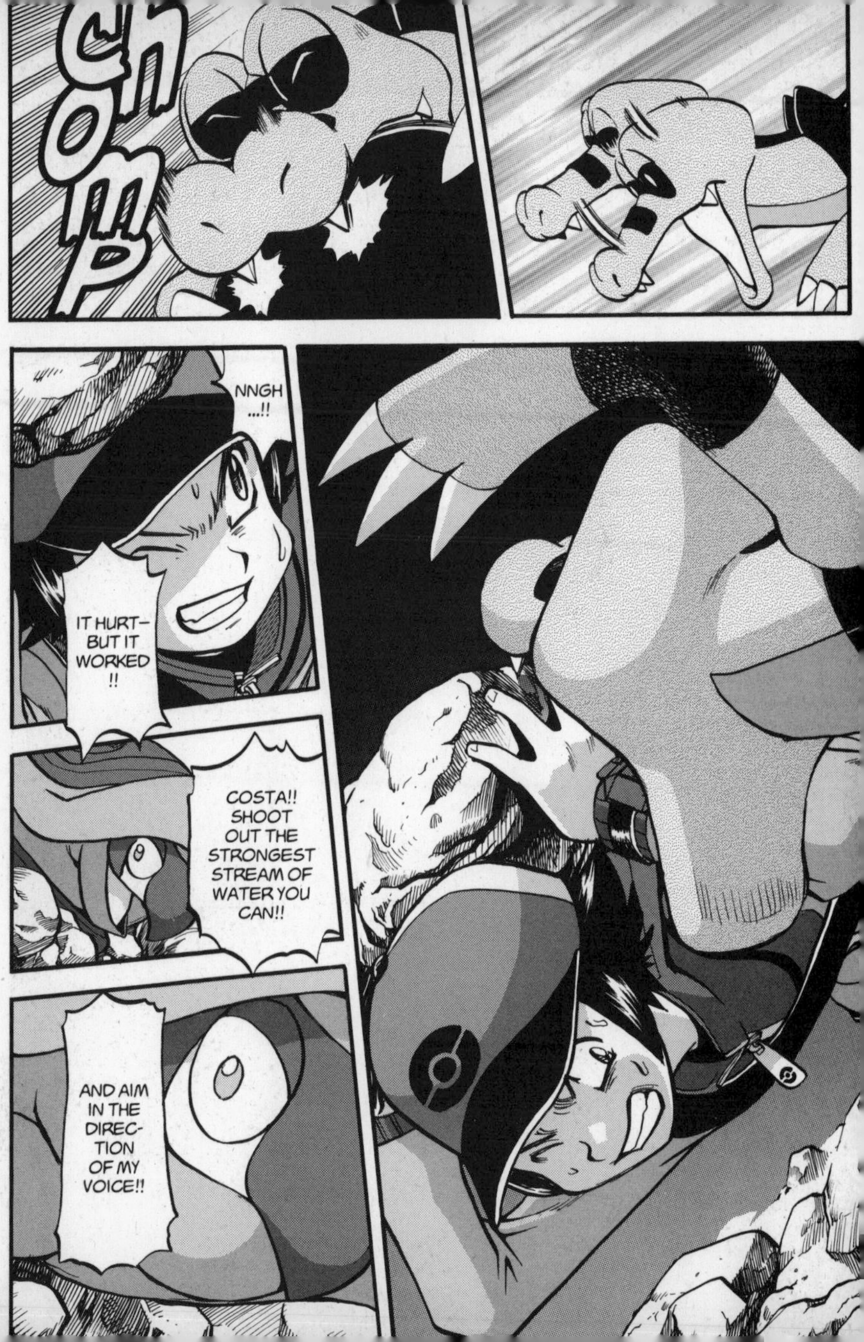
CHOMP
NNGH ...!!
IT HURT—BUT IT WORKED!!
COSTA!! SHOOT OUT THE STRONGEST STREAM OF WATER YOU CAN!!
AND AIM IN THE DIREC-TION OF MY VOICE!!

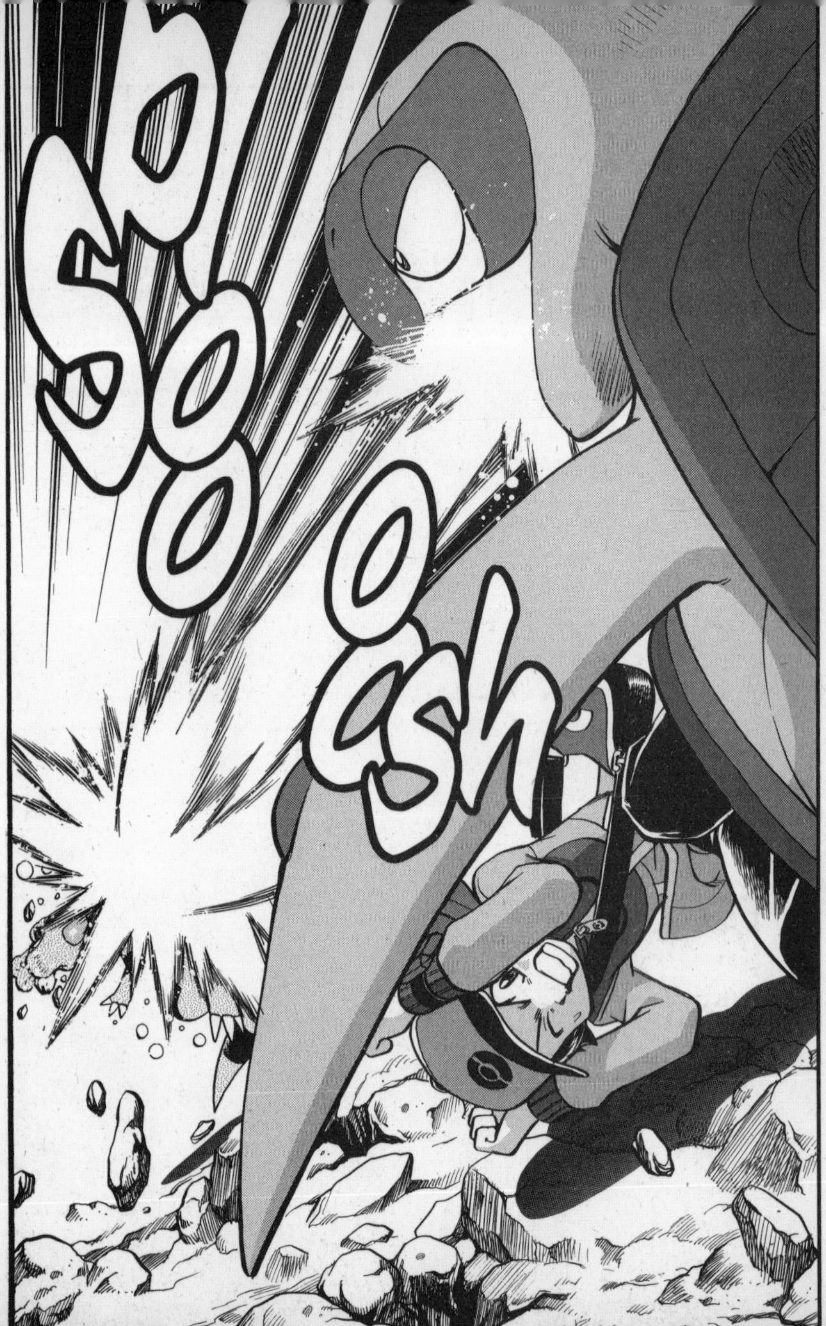
spooosh

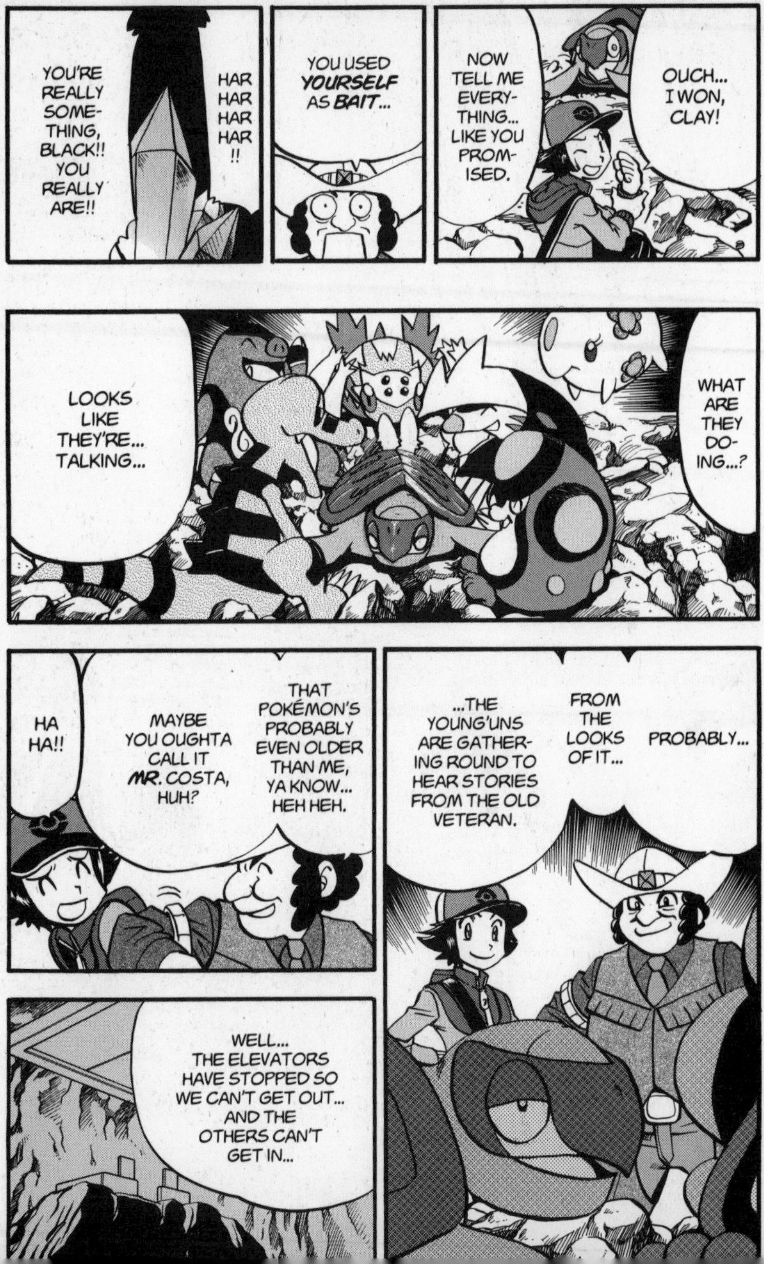
OUCH... I WON, CLAY!
NOW TELL ME EVERYTHING... LIKE YOU PROMISED.
YOU USED **YOURSELF** AS **BAIT**...
HAR HAR HAR HAR!!
YOU'RE REALLY SOMETHING, BLACK!! YOU REALLY ARE!!
WHAT ARE THEY DOING...?
LOOKS LIKE THEY'RE... TALKING...
PROBABLY...
FROM THE LOOKS OF IT...
...THE YOUNG'UNS ARE GATHERING ROUND TO HEAR STORIES FROM THE OLD VETERAN.
THAT POKÉMON'S PROBABLY EVEN OLDER THAN ME, YA KNOW... HEH HEH.
MAYBE YOU OUGHTA CALL IT ***MR.*** COSTA, HUH?
HA HA!!
WELL... THE ELEVATORS HAVE STOPPED SO WE CAN'T GET OUT... AND THE OTHERS CAN'T GET IN...

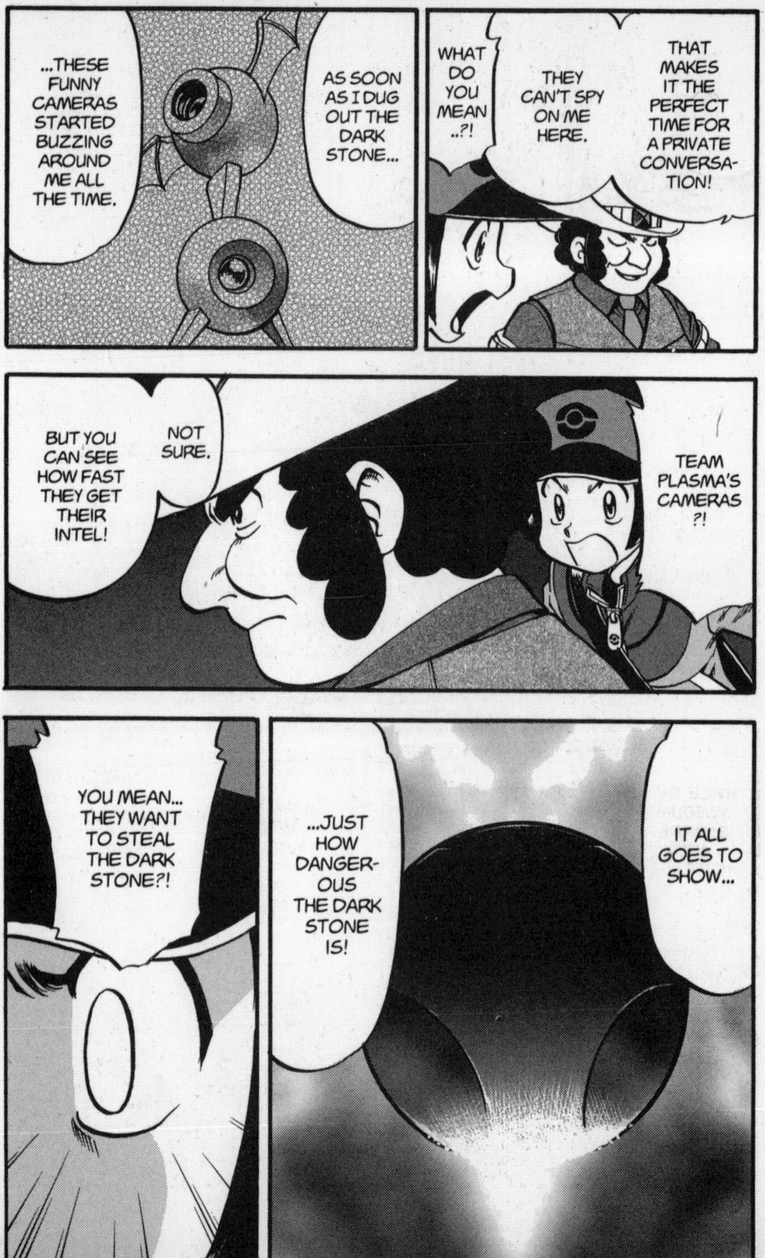
THAT MAKES IT THE PERFECT TIME FOR A PRIVATE CONVERSA-TION!
THEY CAN'T SPY ON ME HERE.
WHAT DO YOU MEAN ..?!
AS SOON AS I DUG OUT THE DARK STONE...
...THESE FUNNY CAMERAS STARTED BUZZING AROUND ME ALL THE TIME.
TEAM PLASMA'S CAMERAS ?!
NOT SURE.
BUT YOU CAN SEE HOW FAST THEY GET THEIR INTEL!
IT ALL GOES TO SHOW...
...JUST HOW DANGER-OUS THE DARK STONE IS!
YOU MEAN... THEY WANT TO STEAL THE DARK STONE?!

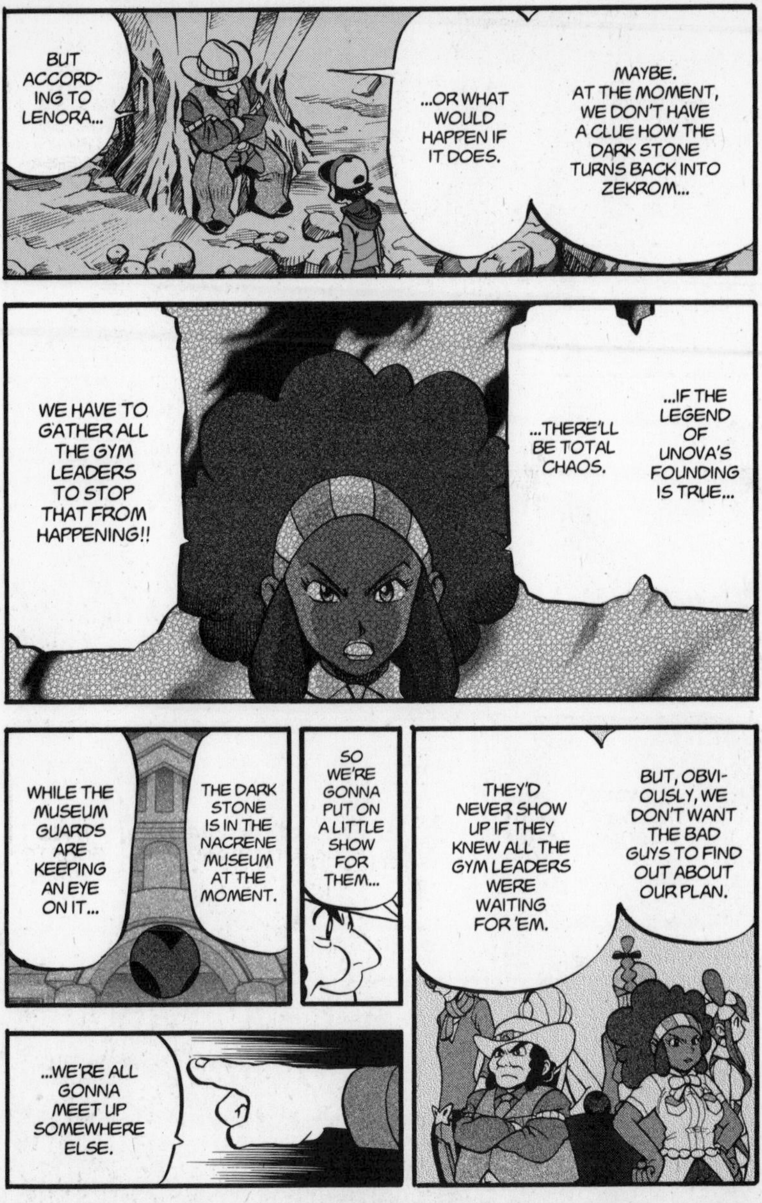
MAYBE. AT THE MOMENT, WE DON'T HAVE A CLUE HOW THE DARK STONE TURNS BACK INTO ZEKROM...
...OR WHAT WOULD HAPPEN IF IT DOES.
BUT ACCORDING TO LENORA...
...IF THE LEGEND OF UNOVA'S FOUNDING IS TRUE...
...THERE'LL BE TOTAL CHAOS.
WE HAVE TO GATHER ALL THE GYM LEADERS TO STOP THAT FROM HAPPENING!!
BUT, OBVIOUSLY, WE DON'T WANT THE BAD GUYS TO FIND OUT ABOUT OUR PLAN.
THEY'D NEVER SHOW UP IF THEY KNEW ALL THE GYM LEADERS WERE WAITING FOR 'EM.
SO WE'RE GONNA PUT ON A LITTLE SHOW FOR THEM...
THE DARK STONE IS IN THE NACRENE MUSEUM AT THE MOMENT.
WHILE THE MUSEUM GUARDS ARE KEEPING AN EYE ON IT...
...WE'RE ALL GONNA MEET UP SOMEWHERE ELSE.

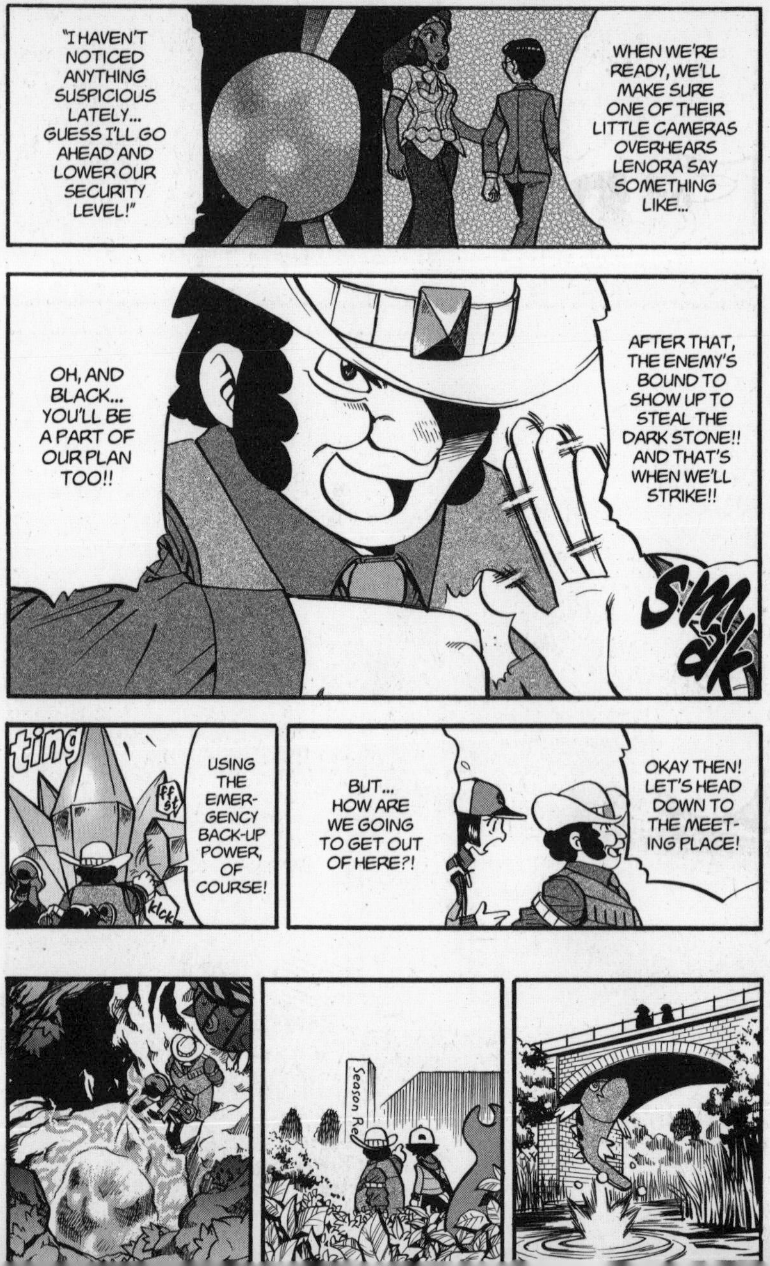
WHEN WE'RE READY, WE'LL MAKE SURE ONE OF THEIR LITTLE CAMERAS OVERHEARS LENORA SAY SOMETHING LIKE...
"I HAVEN'T NOTICED ANYTHING SUSPICIOUS LATELY... GUESS I'LL GO AHEAD AND LOWER OUR SECURITY LEVEL!"
AFTER THAT, THE ENEMY'S BOUND TO SHOW UP TO STEAL THE DARK STONE!! AND THAT'S WHEN WE'LL STRIKE!!
OH, AND BLACK... YOU'LL BE A PART OF OUR PLAN TOO!!
SMak
OKAY THEN! LET'S HEAD DOWN TO THE MEET-ING PLACE!
BUT... HOW ARE WE GOING TO GET OUT OF HERE?!
USING THE EMER-GENCY BACK-UP POWER, OF COURSE!
ting
ffst
klck
Season Re

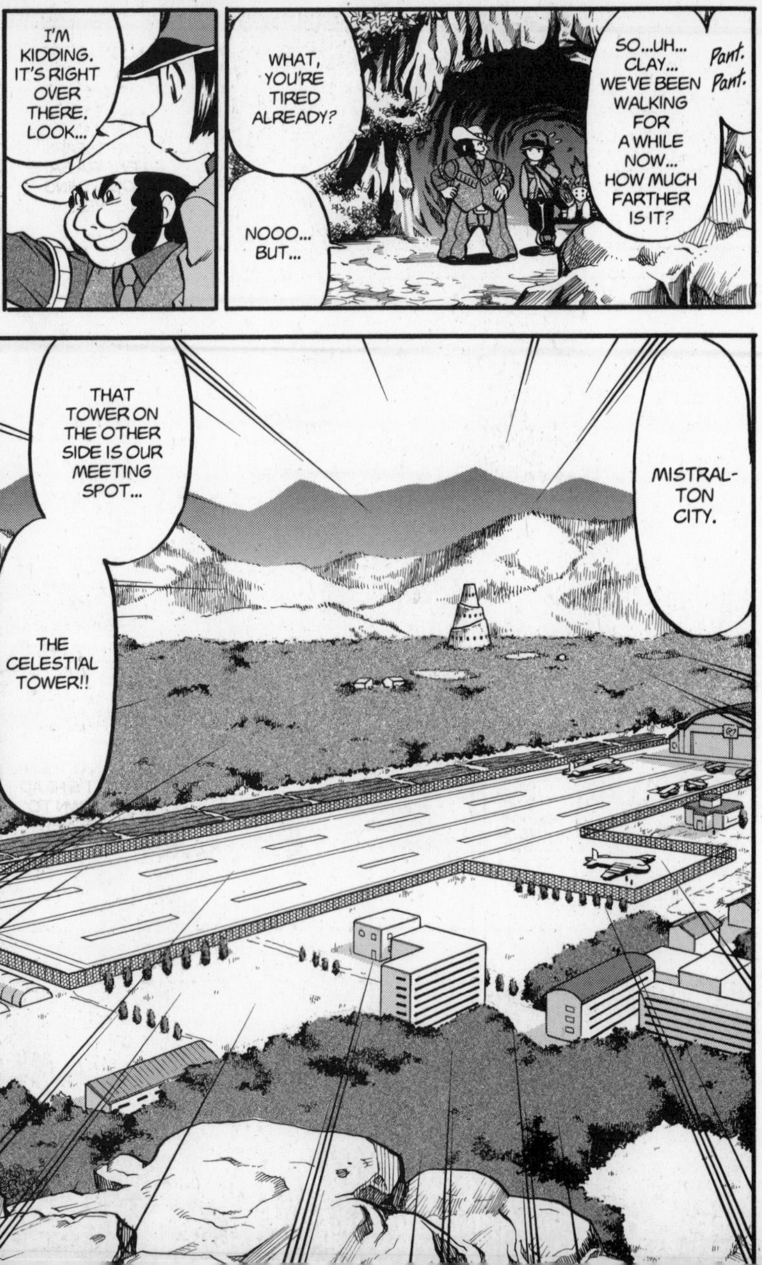
SO...UH... CLAY... WE'VE BEEN WALKING FOR A WHILE NOW... HOW MUCH FARTHER IS IT?
Pant. Pant.
WHAT, YOU'RE TIRED ALREADY?
NOOO... BUT...
I'M KIDDING. IT'S RIGHT OVER THERE. LOOK...
MISTRAL-TON CITY.
THAT TOWER ON THE OTHER SIDE IS OUR MEETING SPOT...
THE CELESTIAL TOWER!!

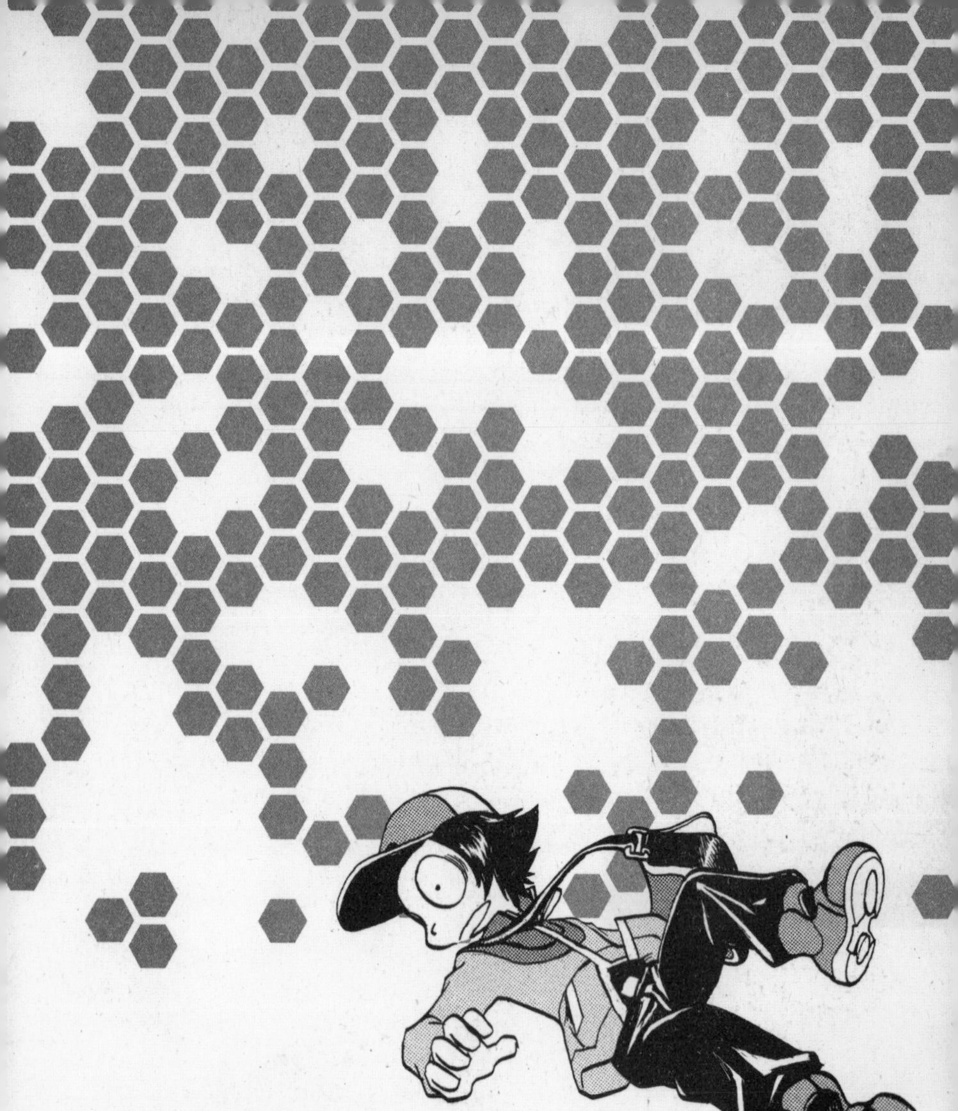

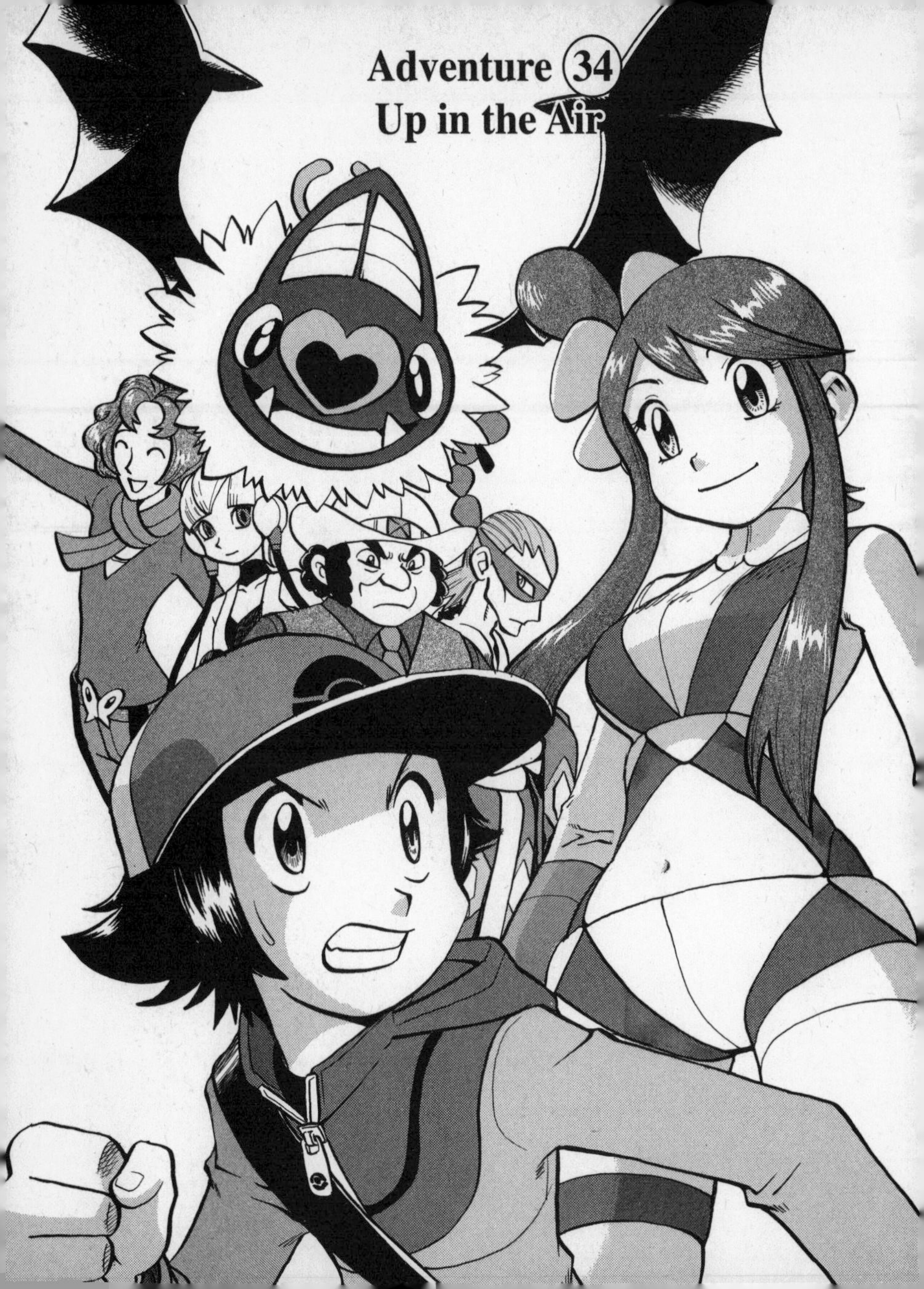
Adventure 34
Up in the Air

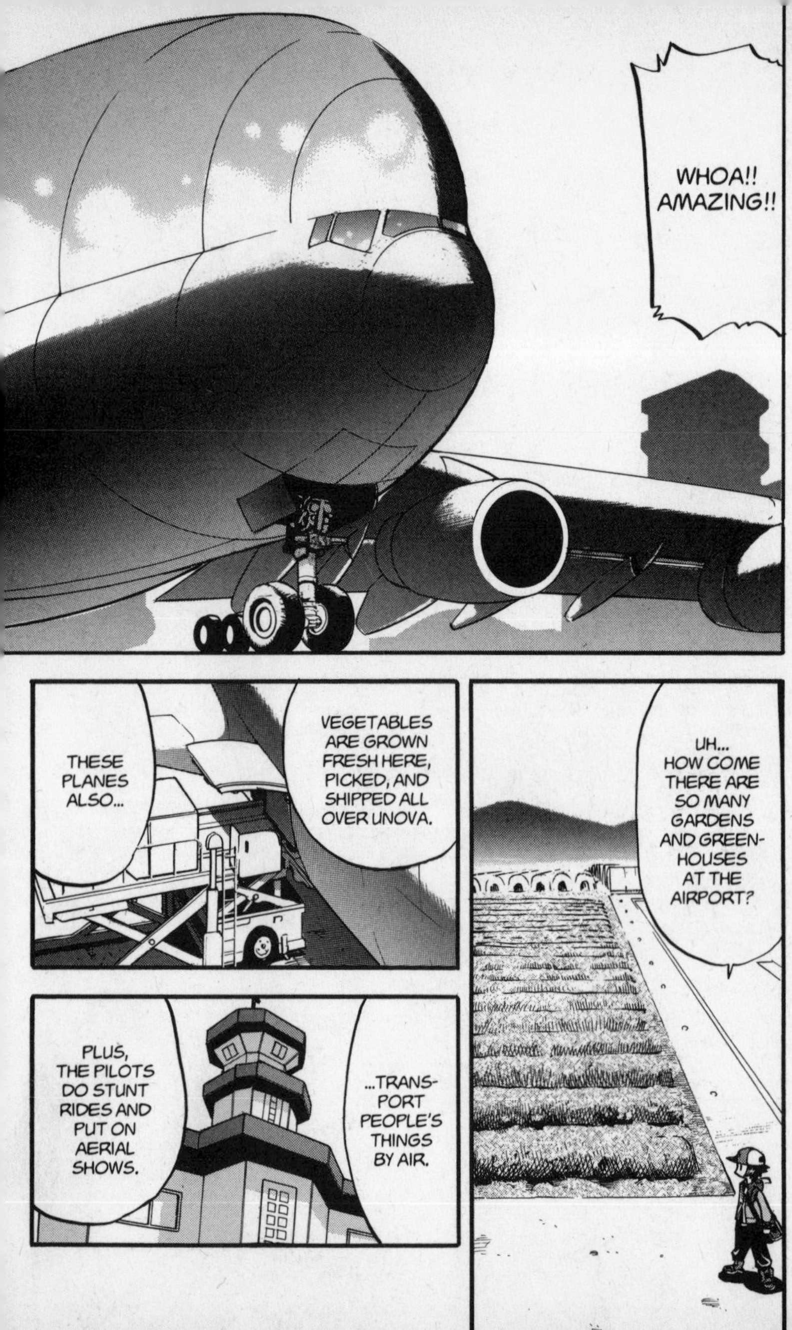
WHOA!! AMAZING!!
UH... HOW COME THERE ARE SO MANY GARDENS AND GREEN-HOUSES AT THE AIRPORT?
VEGETABLES ARE GROWN FRESH HERE, PICKED, AND SHIPPED ALL OVER UNOVA.
THESE PLANES ALSO...
...TRANS-PORT PEOPLE'S THINGS BY AIR.
PLUS, THE PILOTS DO STUNT RIDES AND PUT ON AERIAL SHOWS.

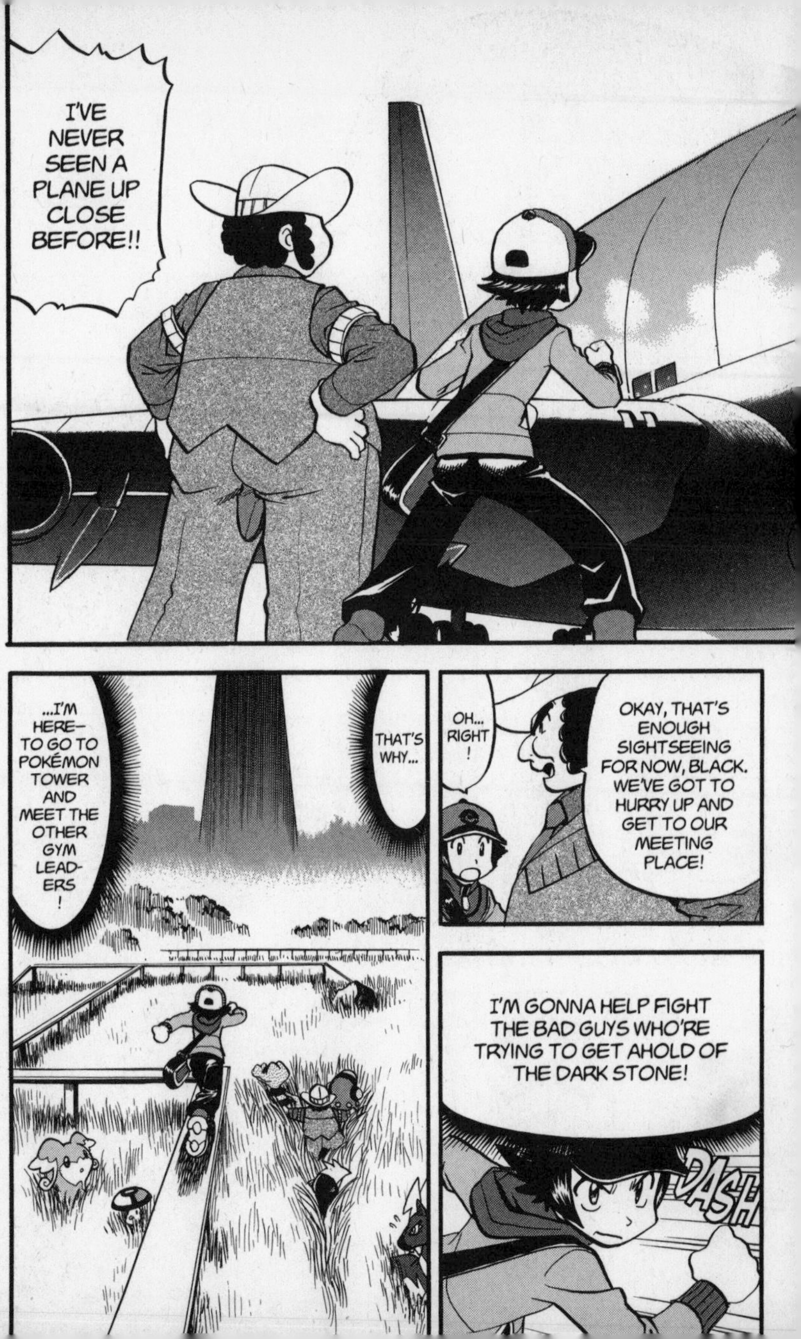
I'VE NEVER SEEN A PLANE UP CLOSE BEFORE!!
OKAY, THAT'S ENOUGH SIGHTSEEING FOR NOW, BLACK. WE'VE GOT TO HURRY UP AND GET TO OUR MEETING PLACE!
OH... RIGHT!
I'M GONNA HELP FIGHT THE BAD GUYS WHO'RE TRYING TO GET AHOLD OF THE DARK STONE!
DASH
THAT'S WHY...
...I'M HERE— TO GO TO POKÉMON TOWER AND MEET THE OTHER GYM LEADERS!

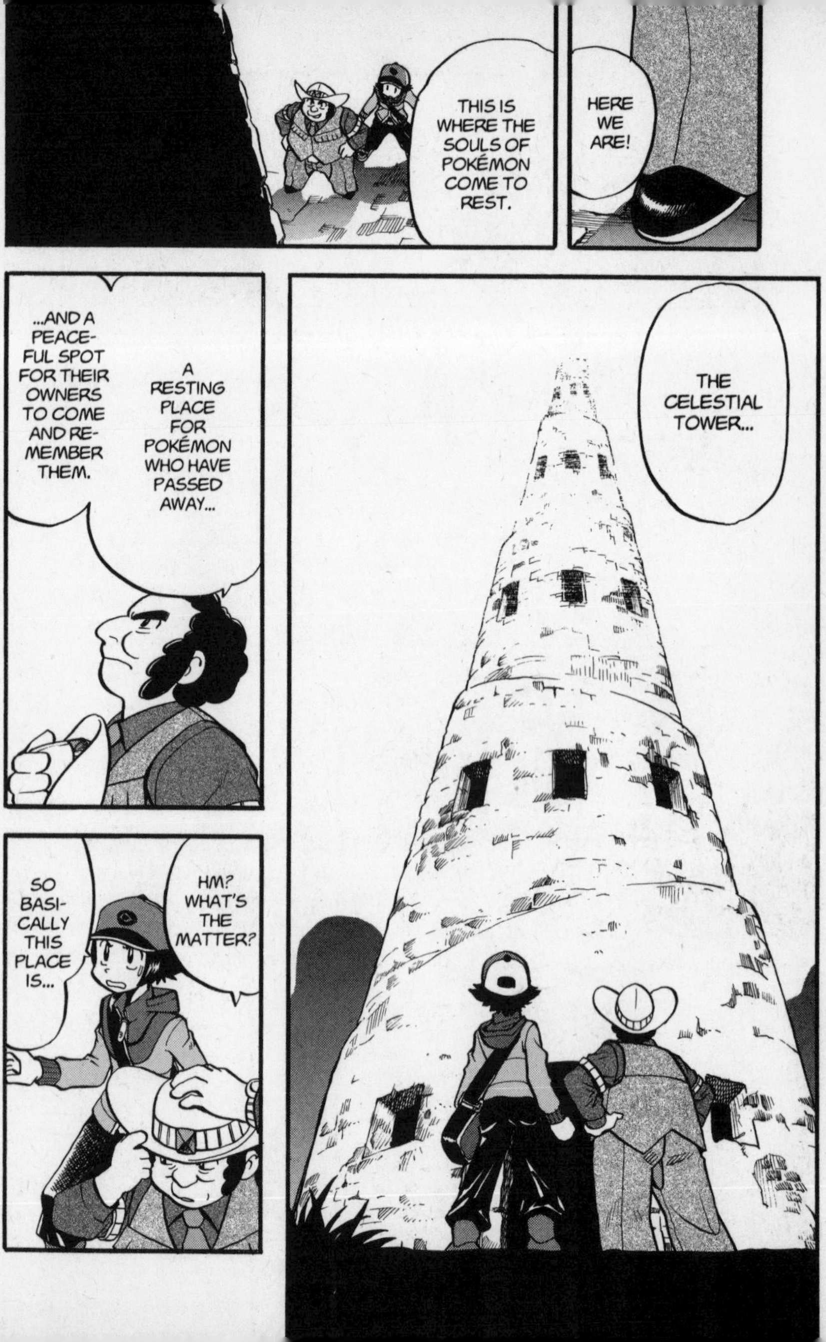
HERE WE ARE!
THIS IS WHERE THE SOULS OF POKÉMON COME TO REST.
THE CELESTIAL TOWER...
A RESTING PLACE FOR POKÉMON WHO HAVE PASSED AWAY...
...AND A PEACEFUL SPOT FOR THEIR OWNERS TO COME AND REMEMBER THEM.
HM? WHAT'S THE MATTER?
SO BASICALLY THIS PLACE IS...

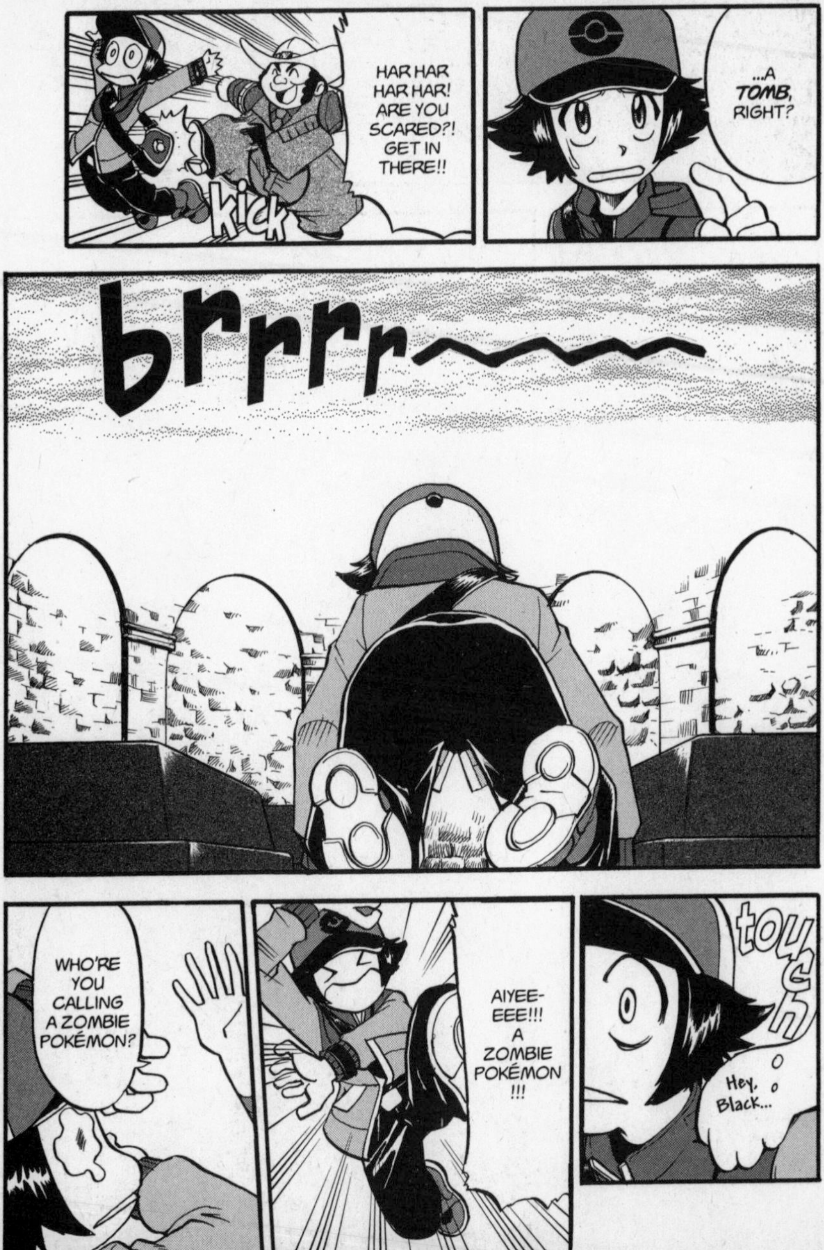
...A TOMB, RIGHT?
HAR HAR HAR HAR! ARE YOU SCARED?! GET IN THERE!!
kick
brrrr
touch
Hey, Black...
AIYEE-EEE!!! A ZOMBIE POKÉMON!!!
WHO'RE YOU CALLING A ZOMBIE POKÉMON?

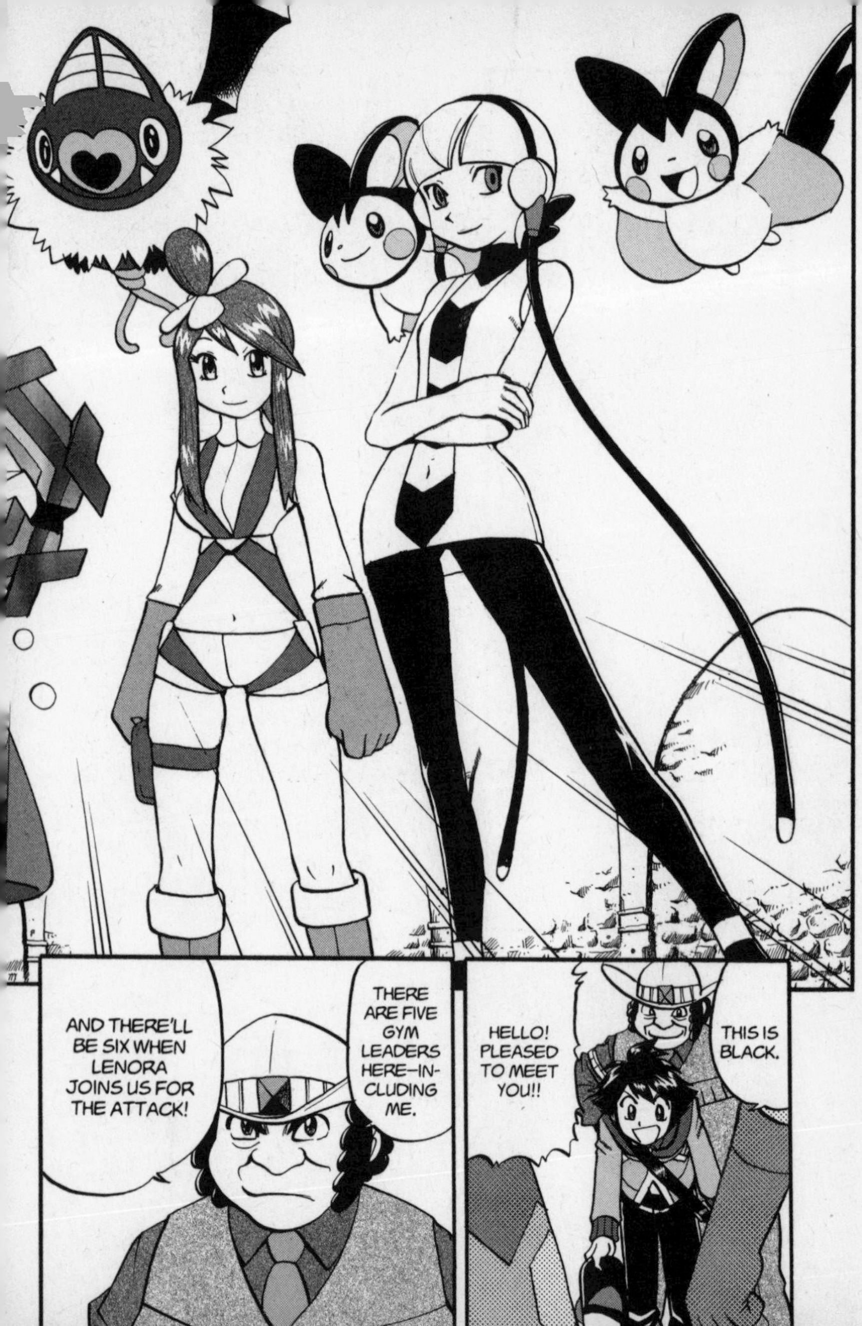
THIS IS BLACK.
HELLO! PLEASED TO MEET YOU!!
THERE ARE FIVE GYM LEADERS HERE—IN-CLUDING ME.
AND THERE'LL BE SIX WHEN LENORA JOINS US FOR THE ATTACK!

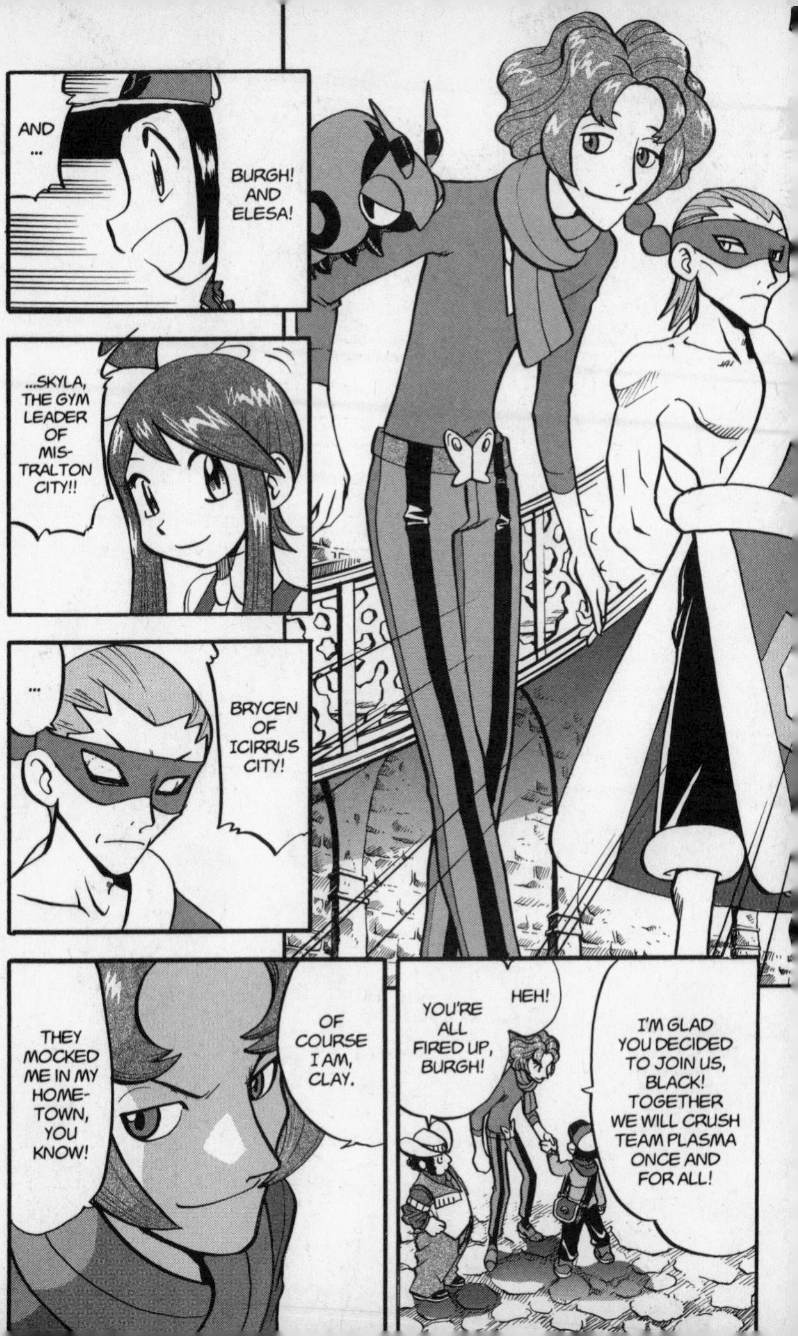
AND ...
BURGH! AND ELESA!
...SKYLA, THE GYM LEADER OF MISTRALTON CITY!!
...
BRYCEN OF ICIRRUS CITY!
I'M GLAD YOU DECIDED TO JOIN US, BLACK! TOGETHER WE WILL CRUSH TEAM PLASMA ONCE AND FOR ALL!
HEH!
YOU'RE ALL FIRED UP, BURGH!
OF COURSE I AM, CLAY.
THEY MOCKED ME IN MY HOMETOWN, YOU KNOW!

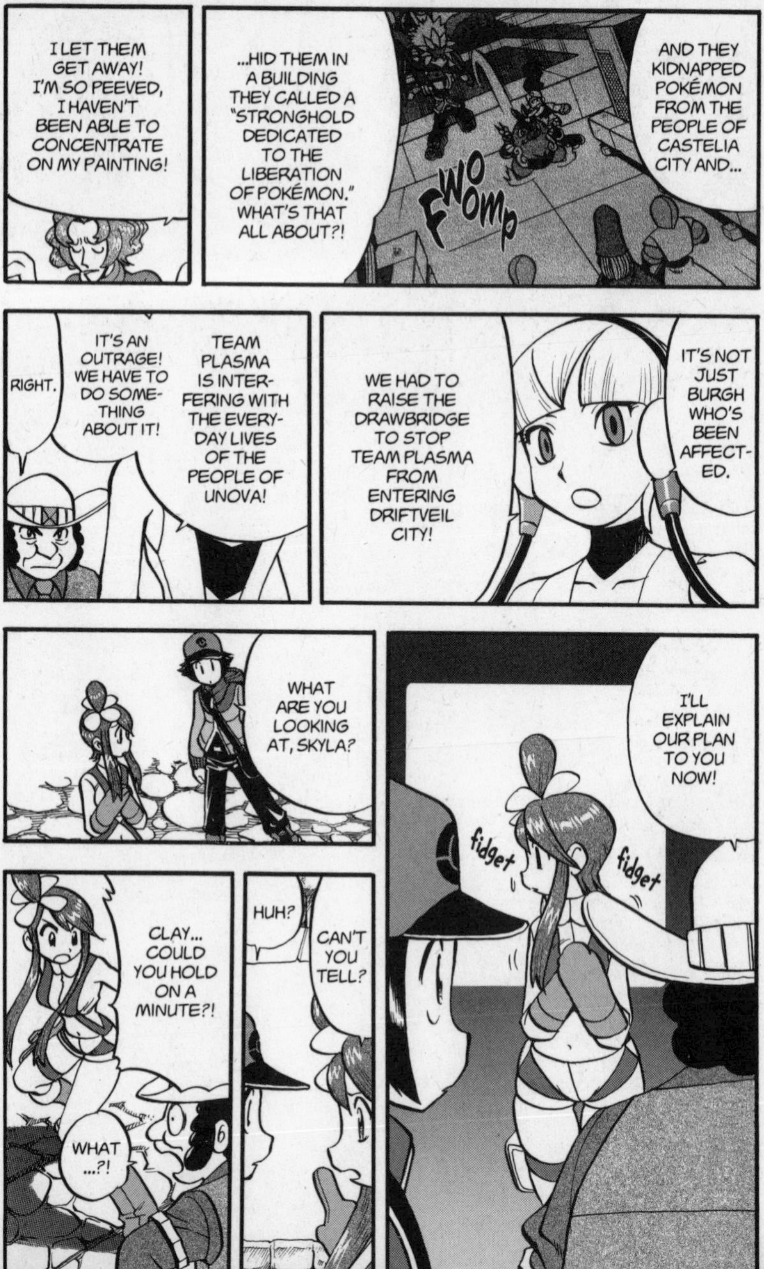
AND THEY KIDNAPPED POKÉMON FROM THE PEOPLE OF CASTELIA CITY AND...
...HID THEM IN A BUILDING THEY CALLED A "STRONGHOLD DEDICATED TO THE LIBERATION OF POKÉMON." WHAT'S THAT ALL ABOUT?!
FWOOMP
I LET THEM GET AWAY! I'M SO PEEVED, I HAVEN'T BEEN ABLE TO CONCENTRATE ON MY PAINTING!
IT'S NOT JUST BURGH WHO'S BEEN AFFECT-ED.
WE HAD TO RAISE THE DRAWBRIDGE TO STOP TEAM PLASMA FROM ENTERING DRIFTVEIL CITY!
TEAM PLASMA IS INTER-FERING WITH THE EVERY-DAY LIVES OF THE PEOPLE OF UNOVA!
IT'S AN OUTRAGE! WE HAVE TO DO SOME-THING ABOUT IT!
RIGHT.
I'LL EXPLAIN OUR PLAN TO YOU NOW!
fidget
fidget
WHAT ARE YOU LOOKING AT, SKYLA?
HUH?
CAN'T YOU TELL?
CLAY... COULD YOU HOLD ON A MINUTE?!
WHAT ...?!

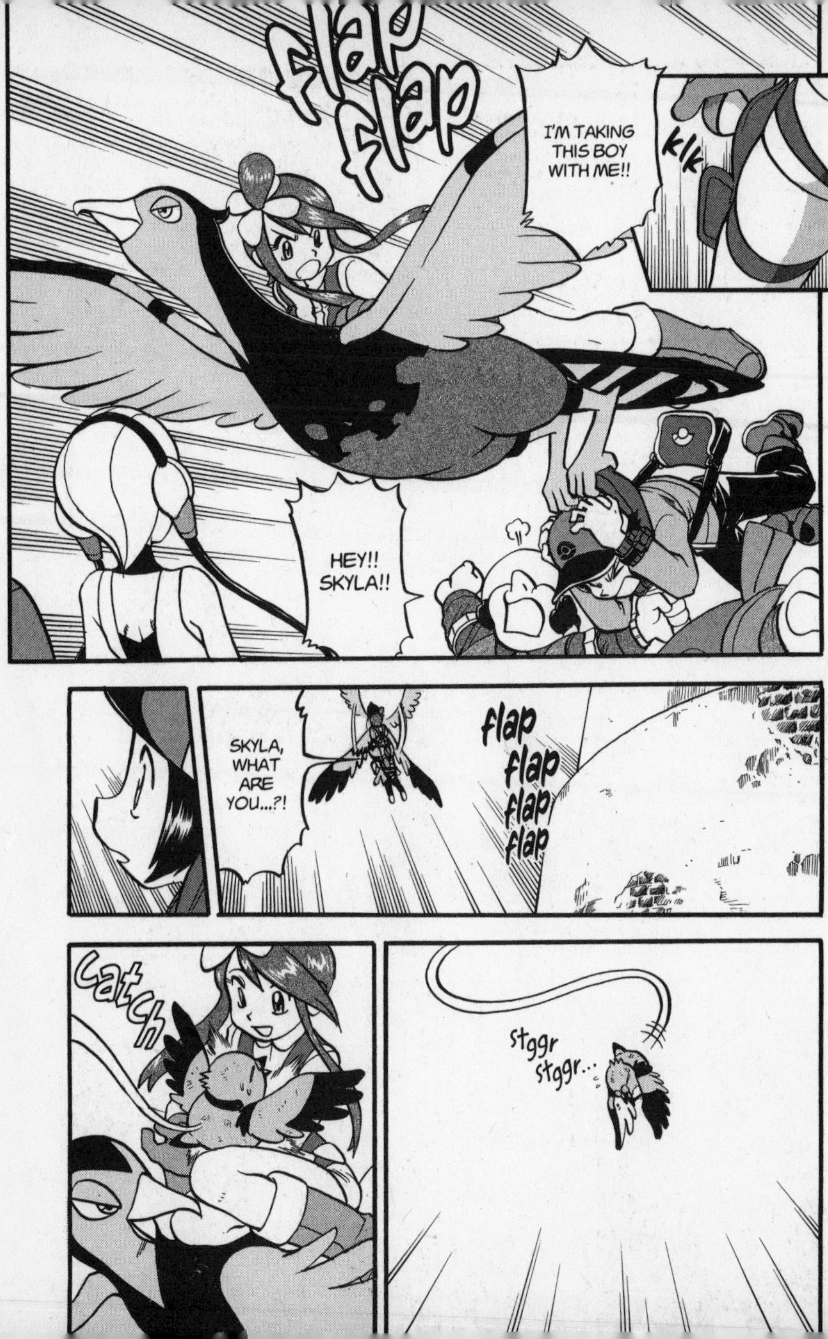
klk
I'M TAKING THIS BOY WITH ME!!
flap flap
HEY!! SKYLA!!
flap flap flap flap
SKYLA, WHAT ARE YOU...?!
stggr stggr...
catch

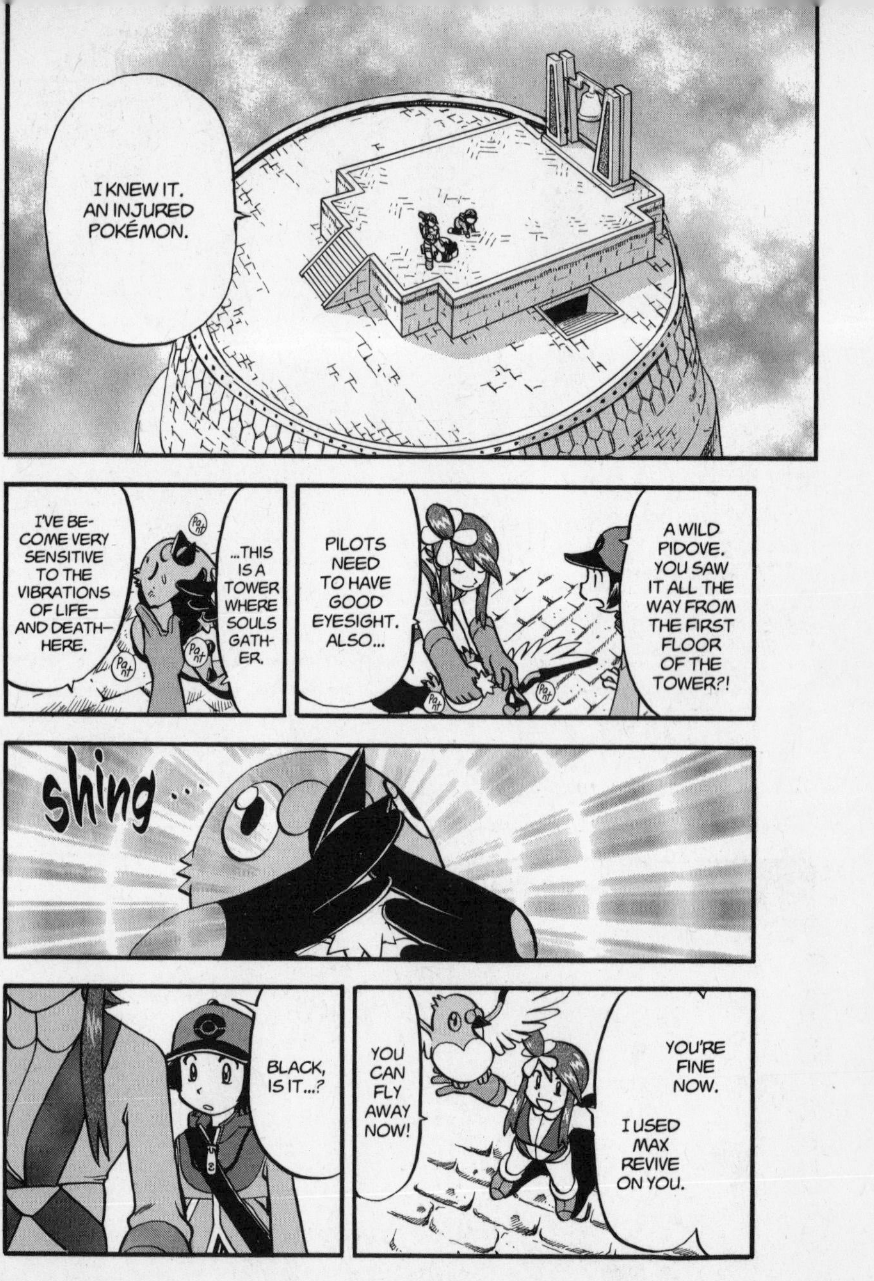
I KNEW IT. AN INJURED POKÉMON.
A WILD PIDOVE. YOU SAW IT ALL THE WAY FROM THE FIRST FLOOR OF THE TOWER?!
PILOTS NEED TO HAVE GOOD EYESIGHT. ALSO...
Pant
Pant
...THIS IS A TOWER WHERE SOULS GATHER.
I'VE BE-COME VERY SENSITIVE TO THE VIBRATIONS OF LIFE—AND DEATH—HERE.
Pant
Pant
Pant
shing...
YOU'RE FINE NOW.
I USED MAX REVIVE ON YOU.
YOU CAN FLY AWAY NOW!
BLACK, IS IT...?

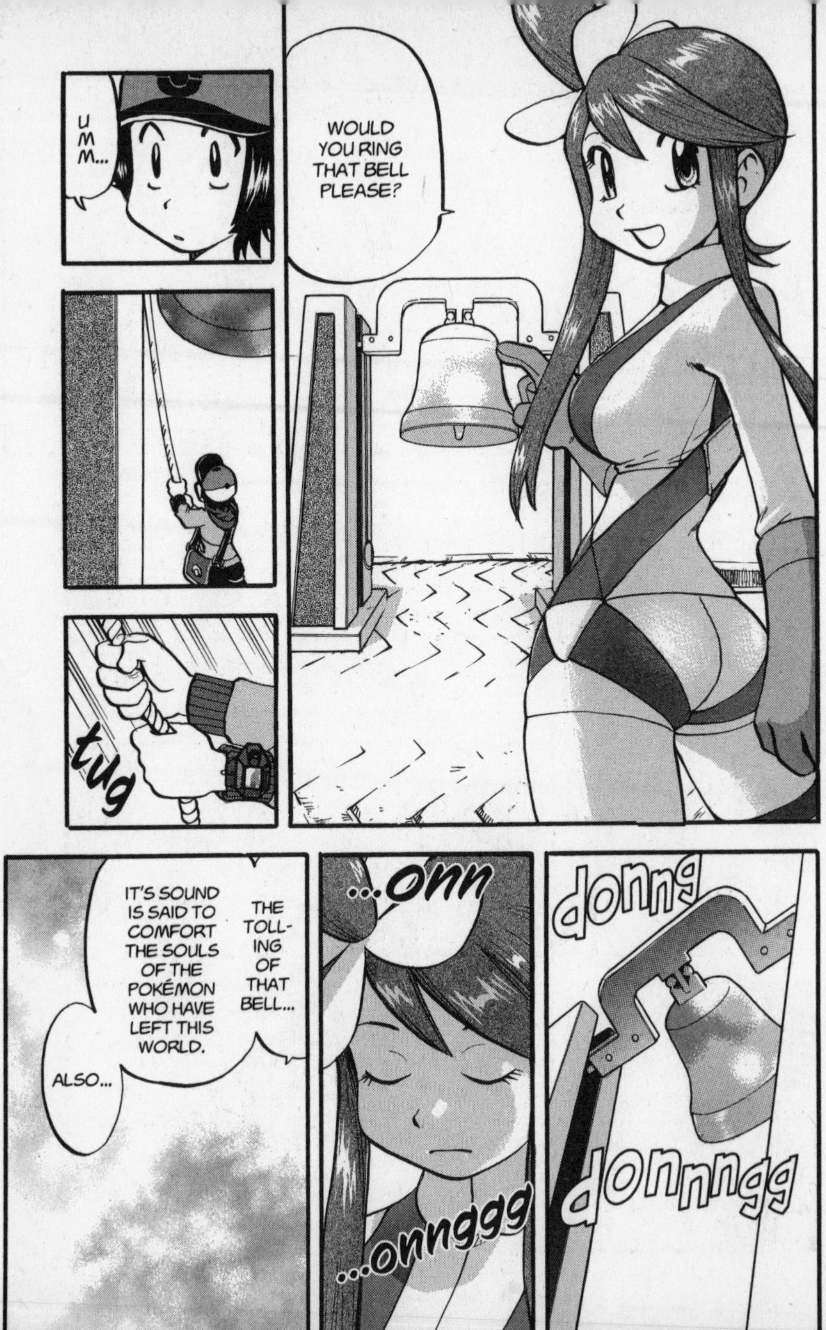
WOULD YOU RING THAT BELL PLEASE?
UMM...
tug
donng
donnngg
...onn
...onnggg
THE TOLLING OF THAT BELL...
IT'S SOUND IS SAID TO COMFORT THE SOULS OF THE POKÉMON WHO HAVE LEFT THIS WORLD.
ALSO...

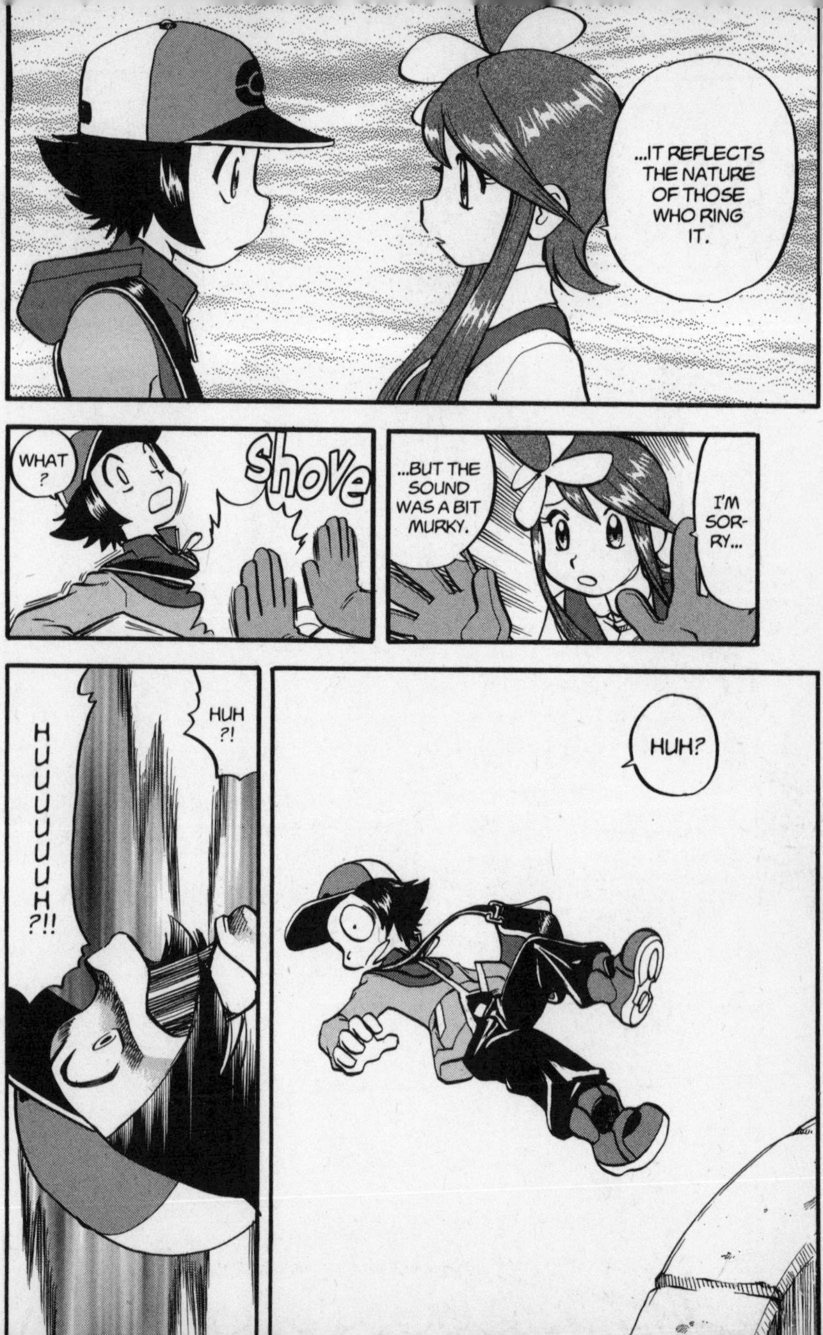
...IT REFLECTS THE NATURE OF THOSE WHO RING IT.
...BUT THE SOUND WAS A BIT MURKY.
I'M SORRY...
shove
WHAT?
HUH?
HUH ?!
HUUUUUUUUH ?!!

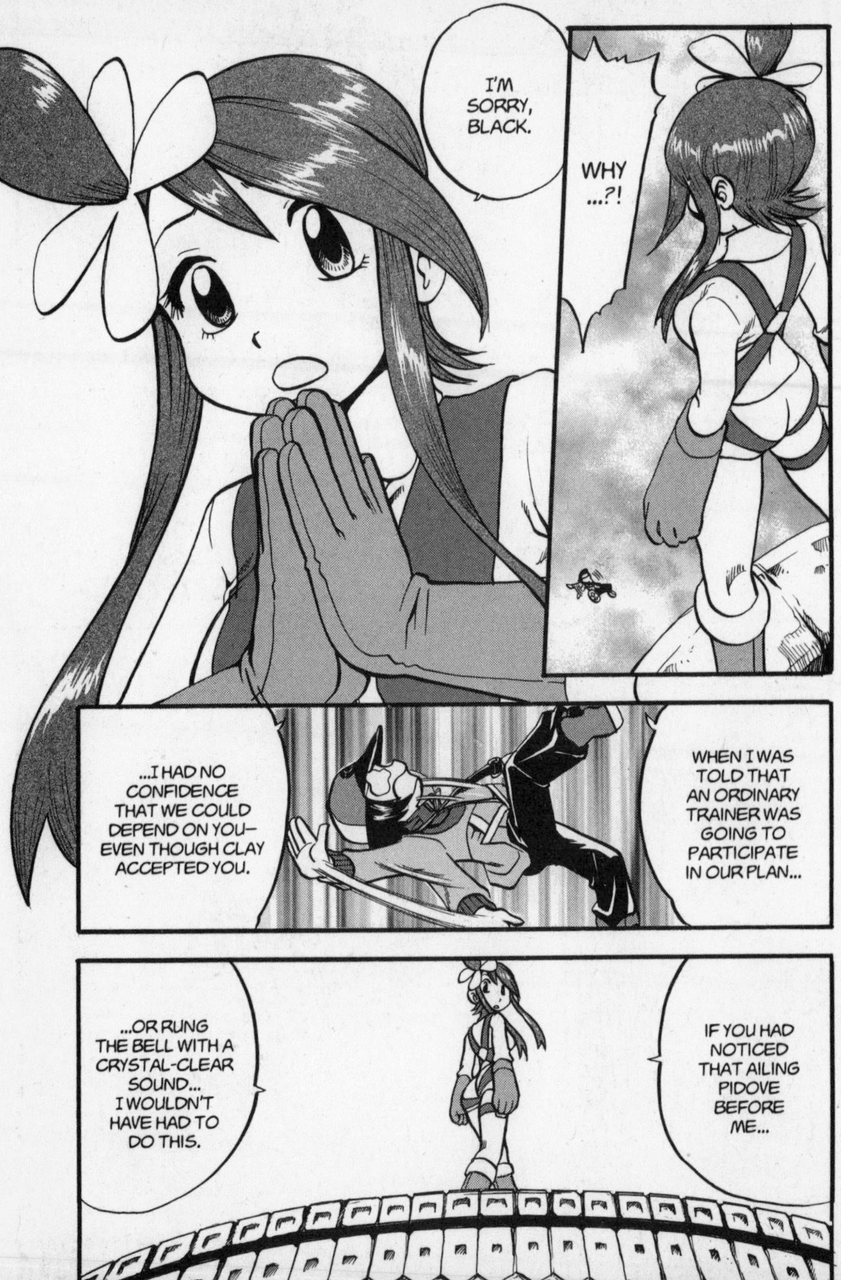
WHY ...?!
I'M SORRY, BLACK.
WHEN I WAS TOLD THAT AN ORDINARY TRAINER WAS GOING TO PARTICIPATE IN OUR PLAN...
...I HAD NO CONFIDENCE THAT WE COULD DEPEND ON YOU—EVEN THOUGH CLAY ACCEPTED YOU.
IF YOU HAD NOTICED THAT AILING PIDOVE BEFORE ME...
...OR RUNG THE BELL WITH A CRYSTAL-CLEAR SOUND... I WOULDN'T HAVE HAD TO DO THIS.

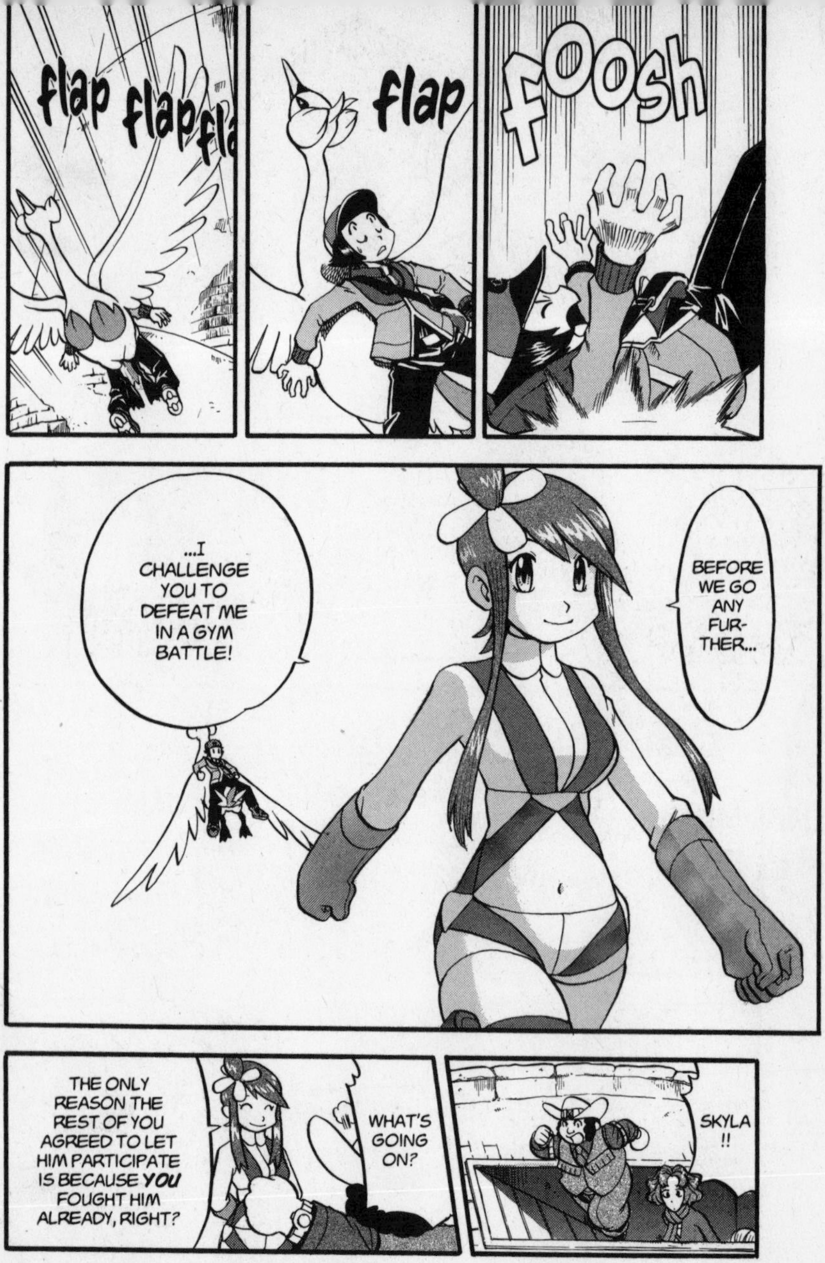
fOOsh
flap
flap flap fla
BEFORE WE GO ANY FUR-THER...
...I CHALLENGE YOU TO DEFEAT ME IN A GYM BATTLE!
SKYLA !!
WHAT'S GOING ON?
THE ONLY REASON THE REST OF YOU AGREED TO LET HIM PARTICIPATE IS BECAUSE *YOU* FOUGHT HIM ALREADY, RIGHT?

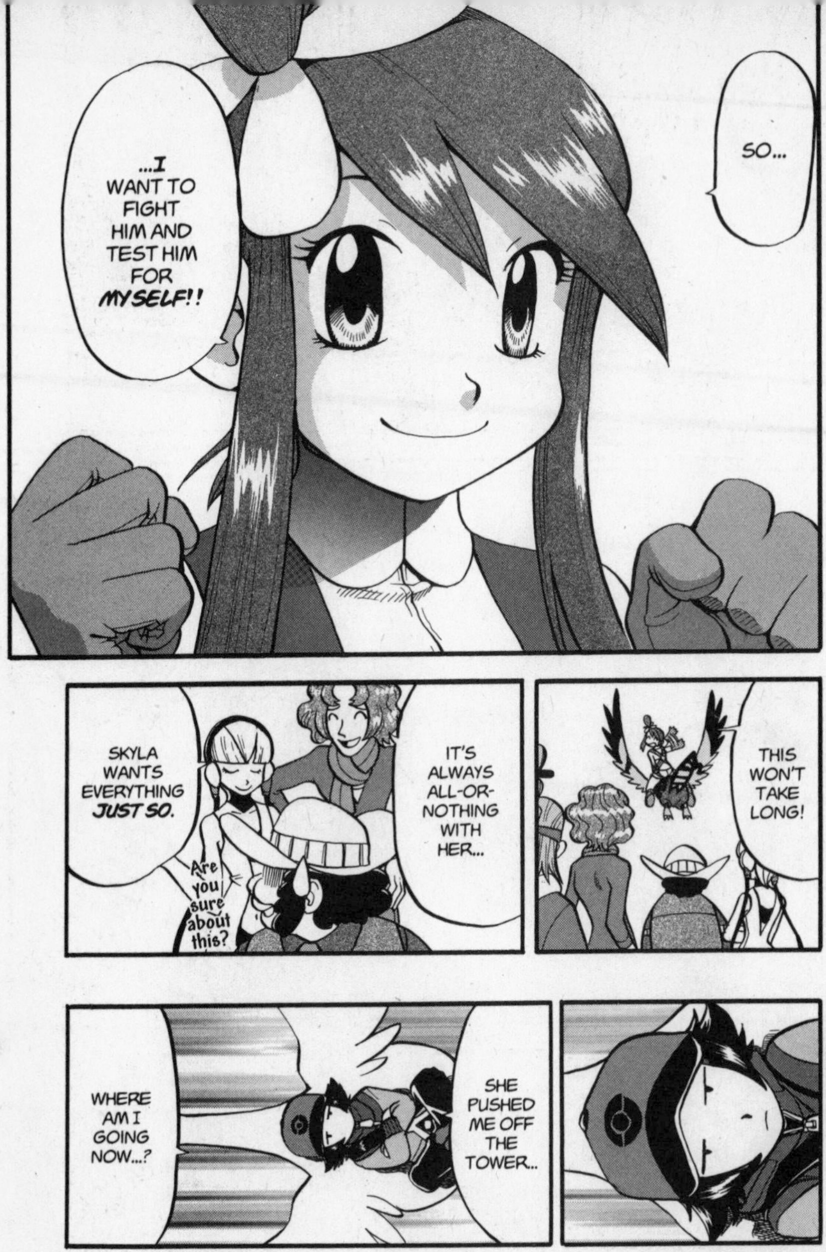
SO...
...I WANT TO FIGHT HIM AND TEST HIM FOR MYSELF!!
THIS WON'T TAKE LONG!
IT'S ALWAYS ALL-OR-NOTHING WITH HER...
SKYLA WANTS EVERYTHING JUST SO.
Are you sure about this?
SHE PUSHED ME OFF THE TOWER...
WHERE AM I GOING NOW...?

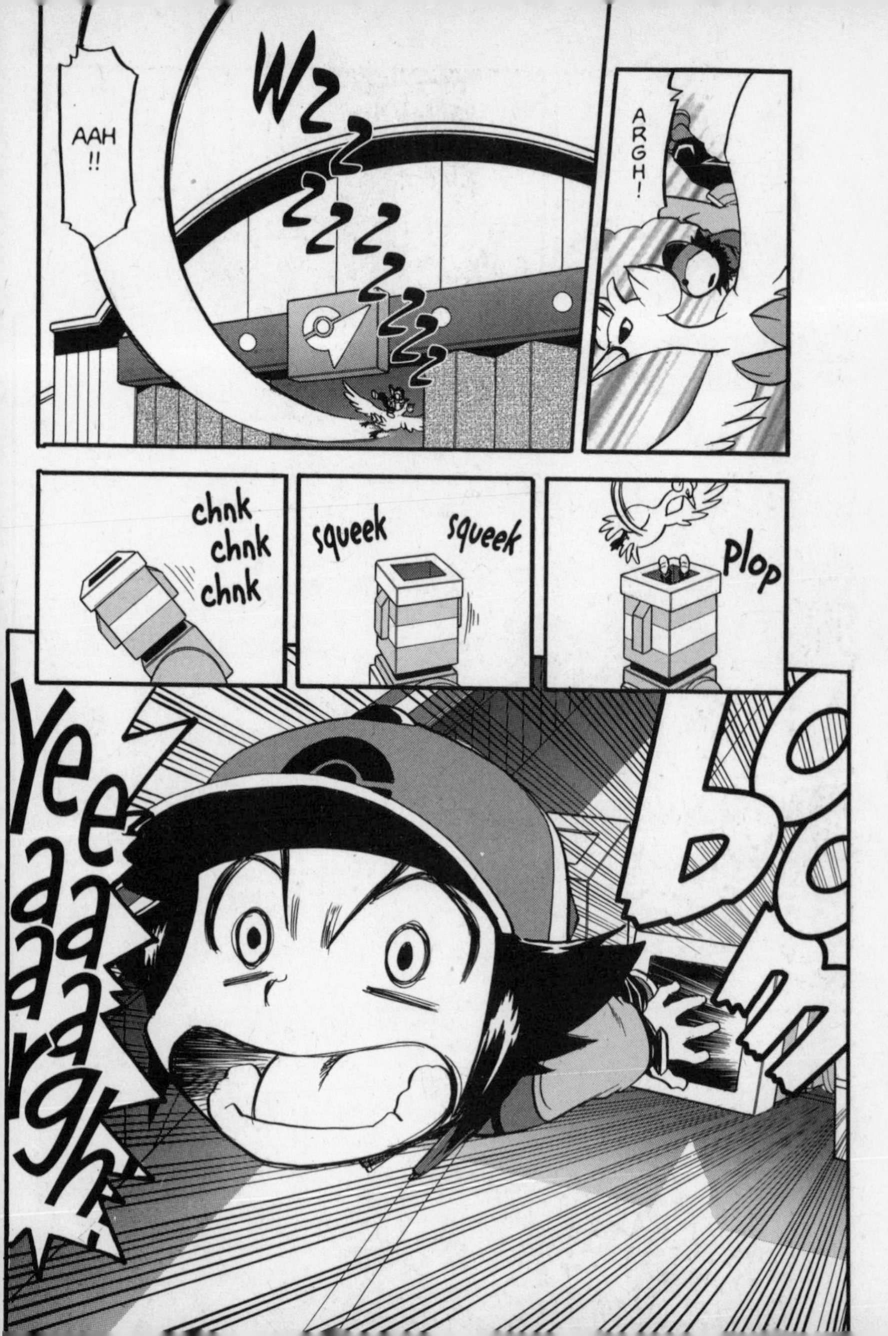
ARGH!
AAH!!
Wzzzzzzzz
plop
squeek
squeek
chnk
chnk
chnk
BOOM
Yeeaaaaargh!

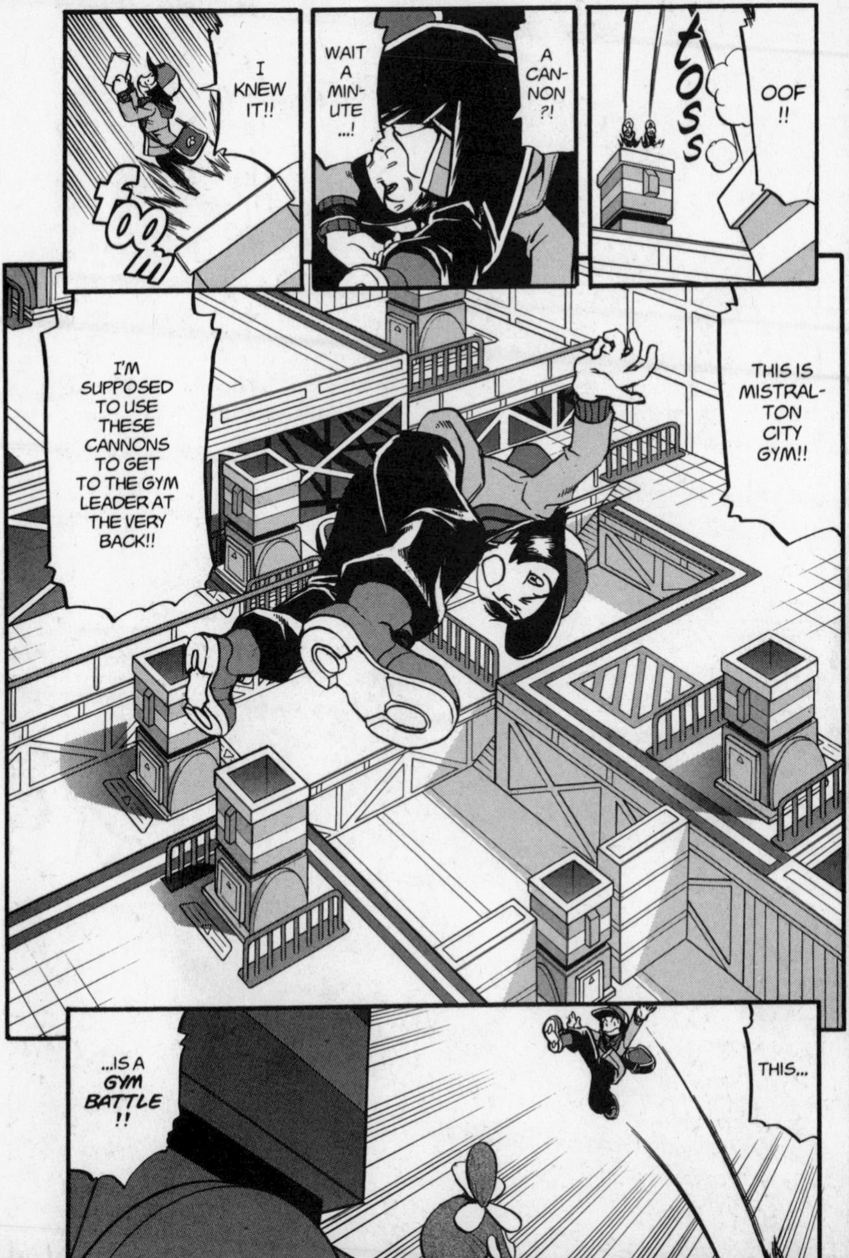
toss
OOF!!
A CAN-NON?!
WAIT A MIN-UTE...!
I KNEW IT!!
foom
THIS IS MISTRAL-TON CITY GYM!!
I'M SUPPOSED TO USE THESE CANNONS TO GET TO THE GYM LEADER AT THE VERY BACK!!
THIS...
...IS A GYM BATTLE!!

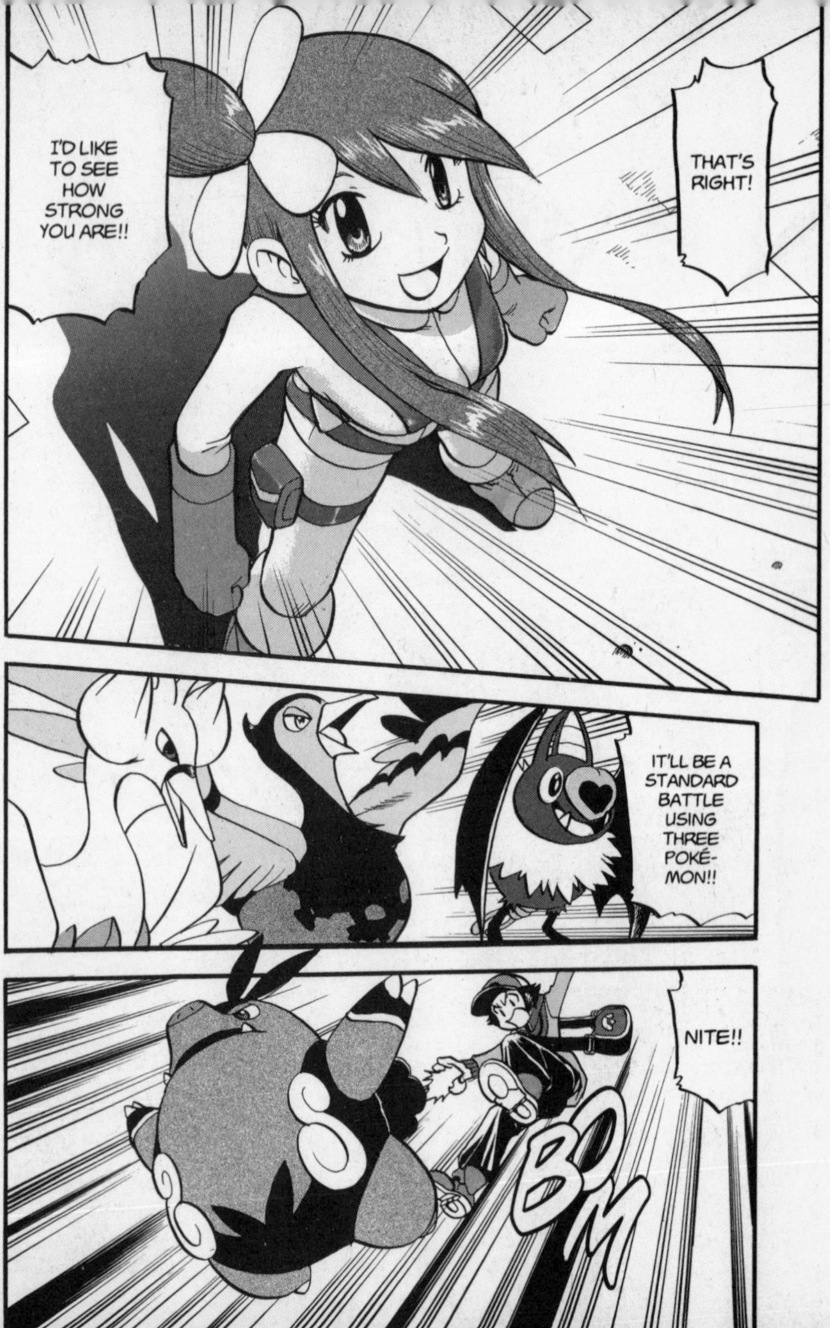
THAT'S RIGHT!
I'D LIKE TO SEE HOW STRONG YOU ARE!!
IT'LL BE A STANDARD BATTLE USING THREE POKÉ-MON!!
NITE!!
BOOM

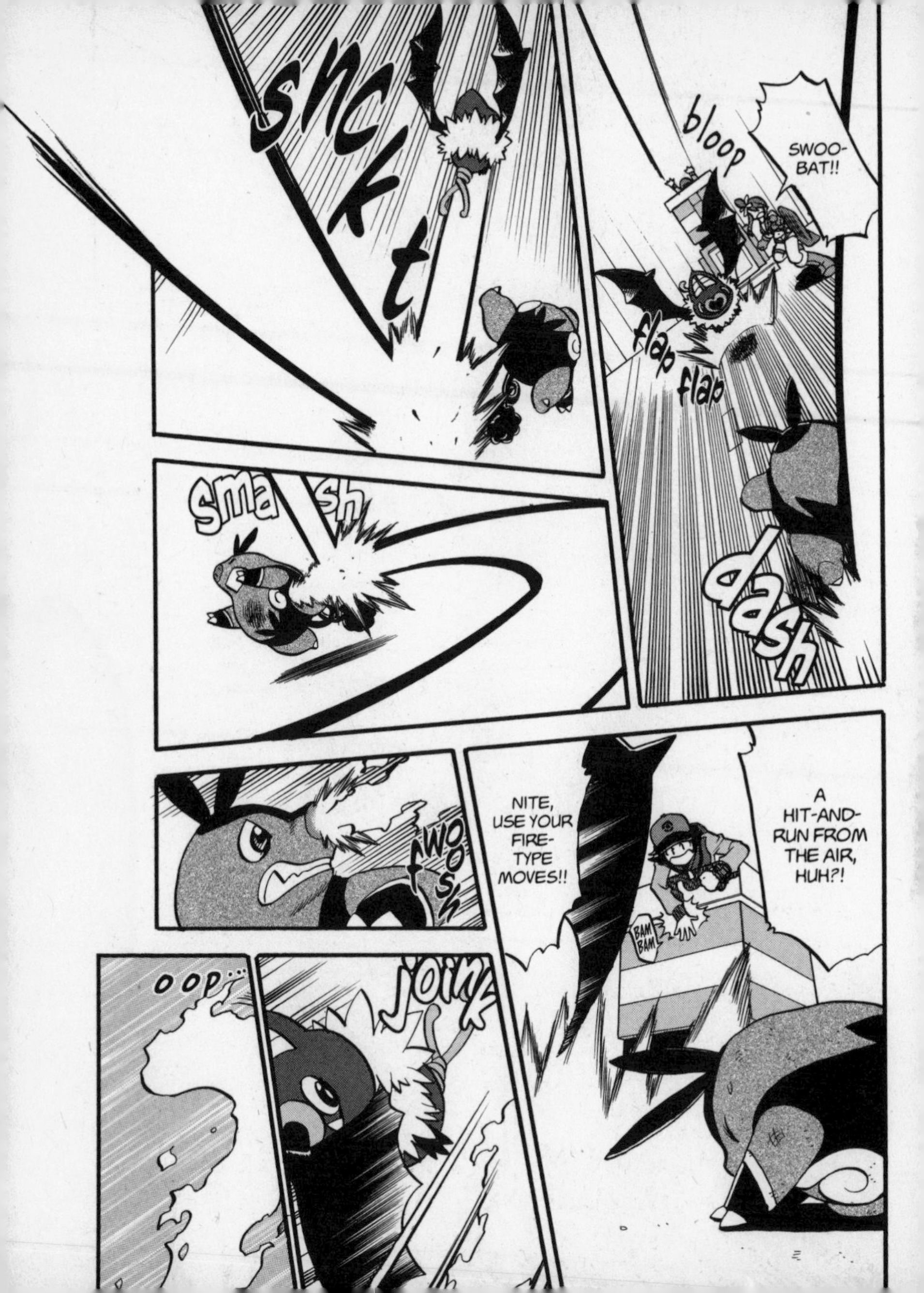
bloop
SWOO-BAT!!
flap
flap
dash
snckt
smash
A HIT-AND-RUN FROM THE AIR, HUH?!
NITE, USE YOUR FIRE-TYPE MOVES!!
BAM BAM
fwoosh
joint
oop...

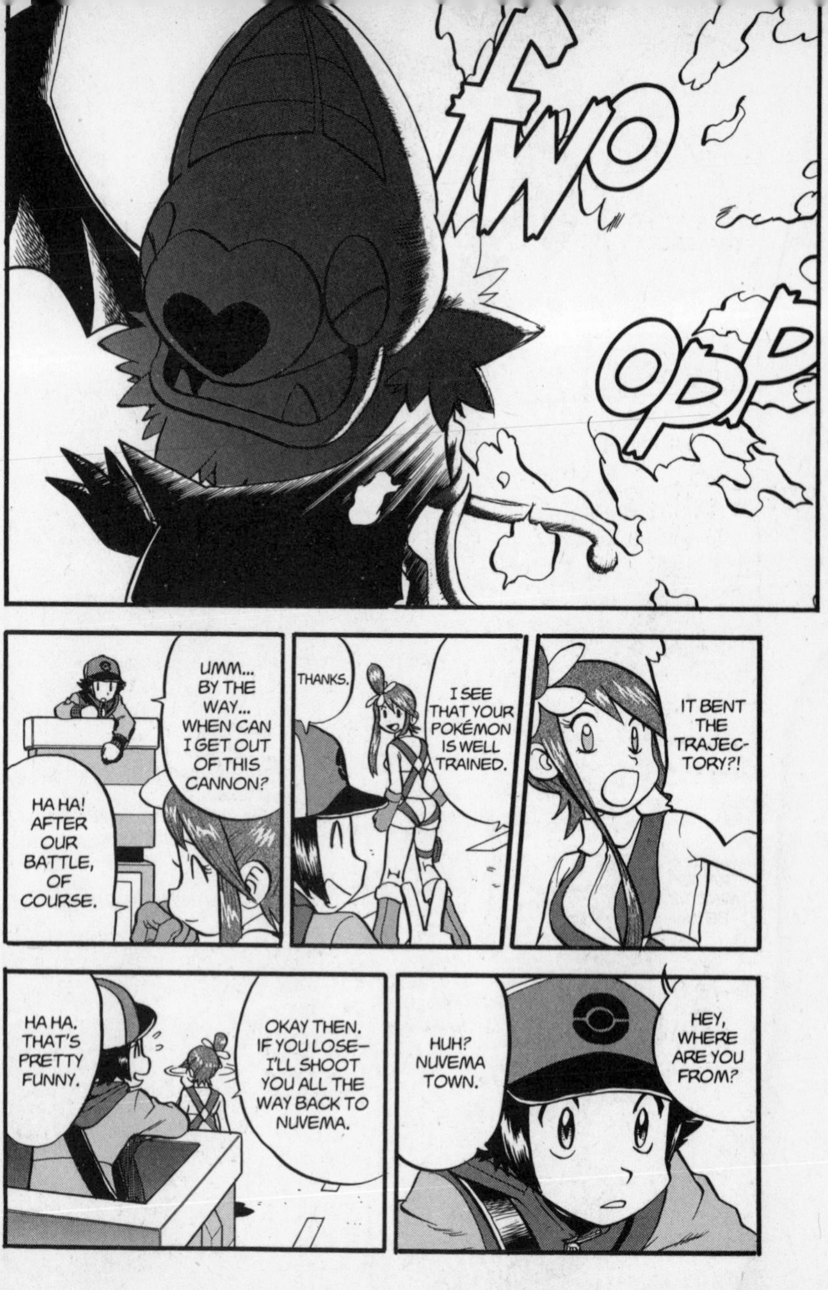
FWOO
IT BENT THE TRAJECTORY?!
I SEE THAT YOUR POKÉMON IS WELL TRAINED.
THANKS.
UMM... BY THE WAY... WHEN CAN I GET OUT OF THIS CANNON?
HA HA! AFTER OUR BATTLE, OF COURSE.
HEY, WHERE ARE YOU FROM?
HUH? NUVEMA TOWN.
OKAY THEN. IF YOU LOSE— I'LL SHOOT YOU ALL THE WAY BACK TO NUVEMA.
HA HA. THAT'S PRETTY FUNNY.

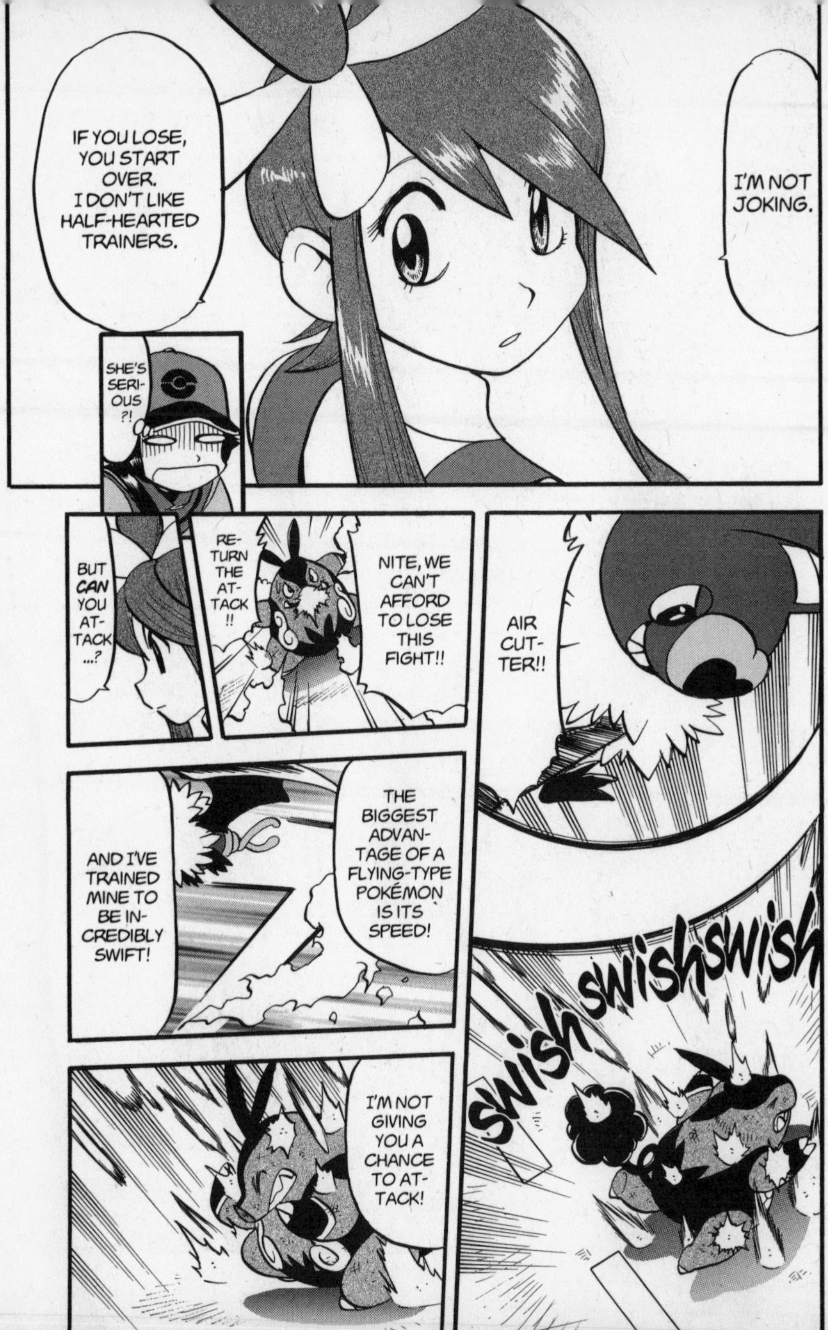
IF YOU LOSE, YOU START OVER. I DON'T LIKE HALF-HEARTED TRAINERS.
I'M NOT JOKING.
SHE'S SERIOUS ?!
AIR CUTTER!!
swish swishswish
NITE, WE CAN'T AFFORD TO LOSE THIS FIGHT!!
RETURN THE ATTACK!!
BUT **CAN** YOU ATTACK ...?
THE BIGGEST ADVANTAGE OF A FLYING-TYPE POKÉMON IS ITS SPEED!
AND I'VE TRAINED MINE TO BE INCREDIBLY SWIFT!
I'M NOT GIVING YOU A CHANCE TO ATTACK!

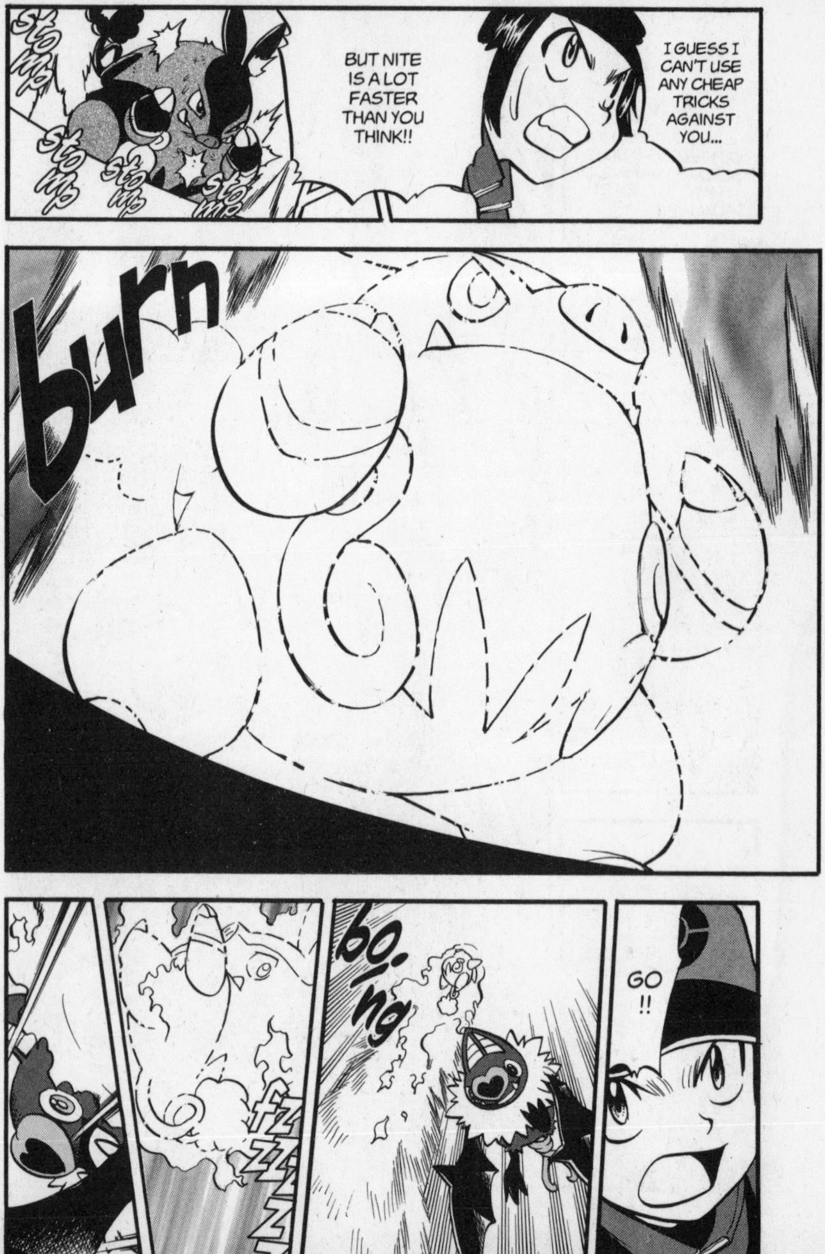

I GUESS I CAN'T USE ANY CHEAP TRICKS AGAINST YOU...
BUT NITE IS A LOT FASTER THAN YOU THINK!!
stomp
stomp
stomp
stomp
burn
GO !!
boing
fzzzzz

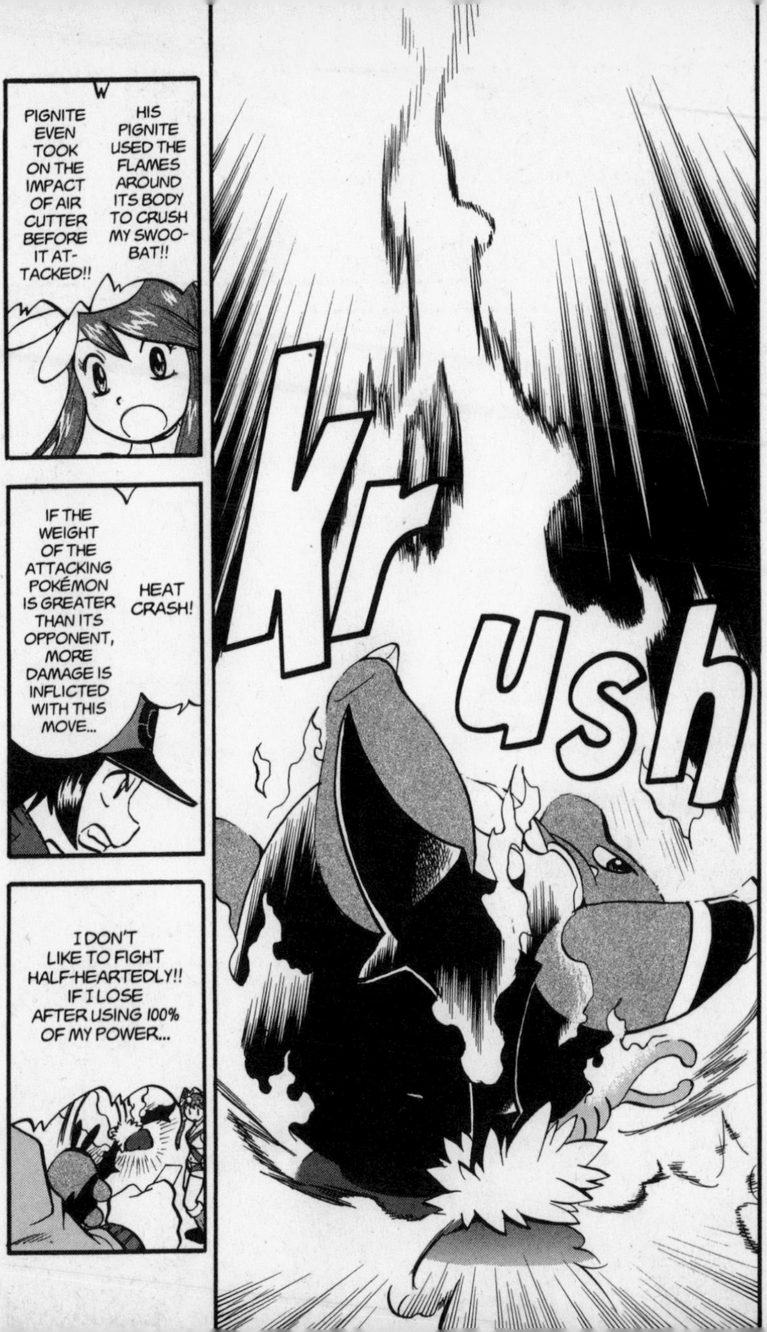
Kr
ush
HIS PIGNITE USED THE FLAMES AROUND ITS BODY TO CRUSH MY SWOO-BAT!!
PIGNITE EVEN TOOK ON THE IMPACT OF AIR CUTTER BEFORE IT AT-TACKED!!
HEAT CRASH!
IF THE WEIGHT OF THE ATTACKING POKÉMON IS GREATER THAN ITS OPPONENT, MORE DAMAGE IS INFLICTED WITH THIS MOVE...
I DON'T LIKE TO FIGHT HALF-HEARTEDLY!! IF I LOSE AFTER USING 100% OF MY POWER...

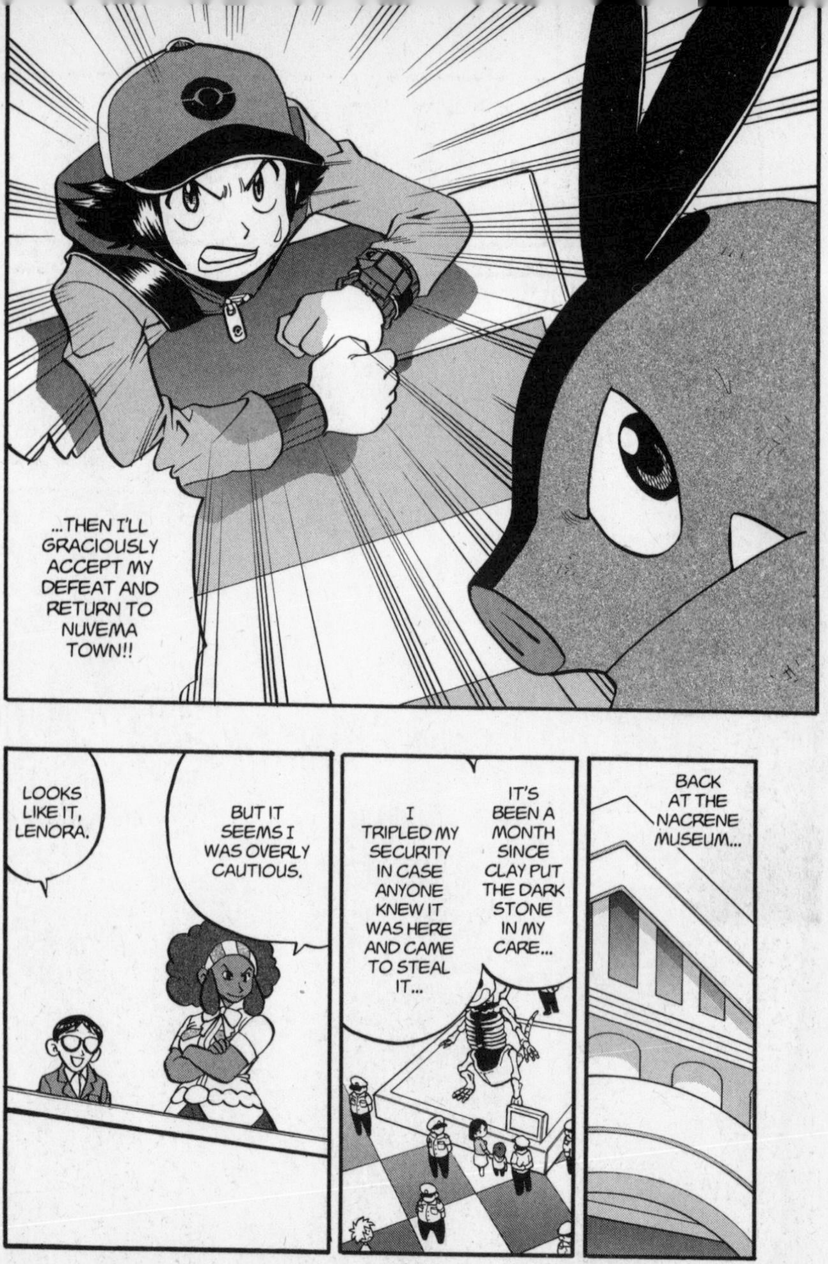
...THEN I'LL GRACIOUSLY ACCEPT MY DEFEAT AND RETURN TO NUVEMA TOWN!!
BACK AT THE NACRENE MUSEUM...
IT'S BEEN A MONTH SINCE CLAY PUT THE DARK STONE IN MY CARE...
I TRIPLED MY SECURITY IN CASE ANYONE KNEW IT WAS HERE AND CAME TO STEAL IT...
BUT IT SEEMS I WAS OVERLY CAUTIOUS.
LOOKS LIKE IT, LENORA.

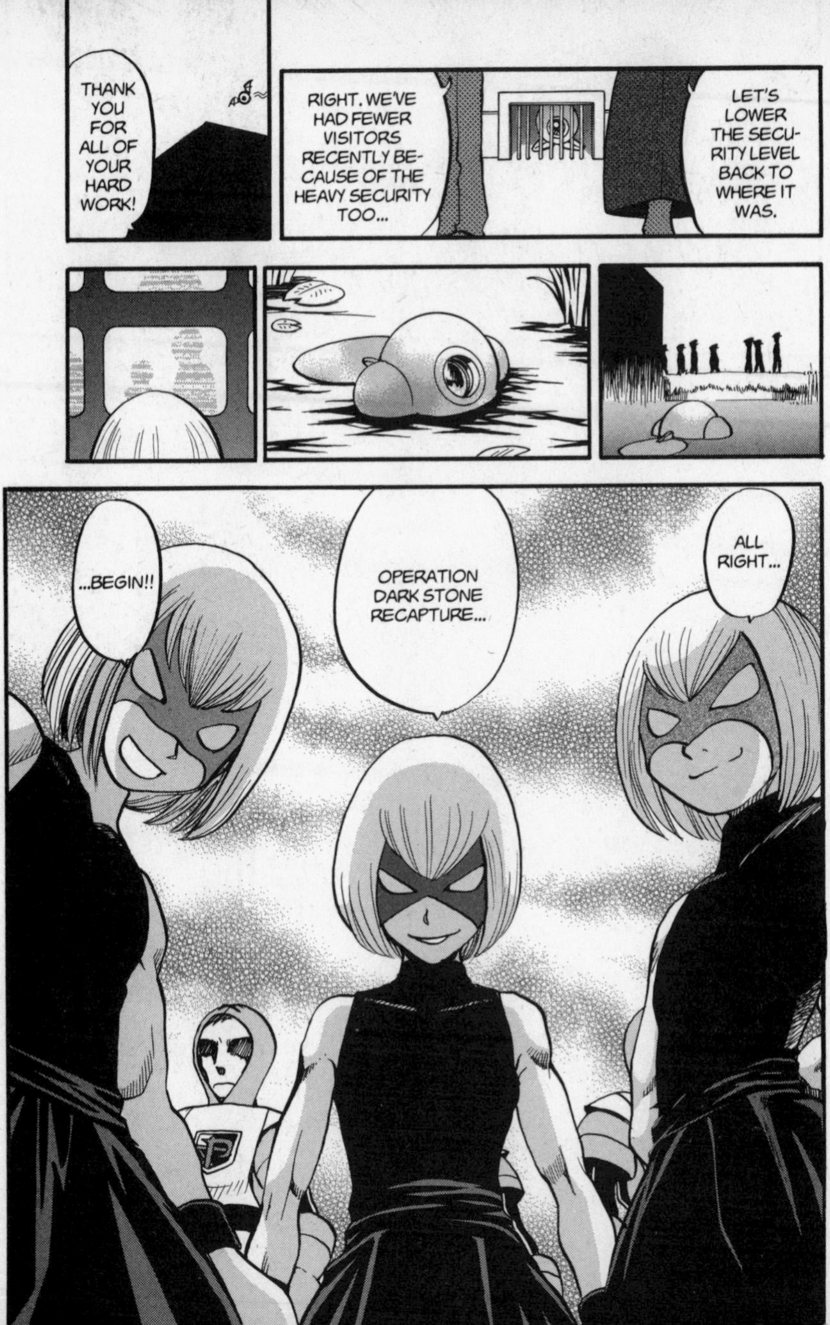
LET'S LOWER THE SECURITY LEVEL BACK TO WHERE IT WAS.
RIGHT. WE'VE HAD FEWER VISITORS RECENTLY BECAUSE OF THE HEAVY SECURITY TOO...
THANK YOU FOR ALL OF YOUR HARD WORK!
ALL RIGHT...
OPERATION DARK STONE RECAPTURE...
...BEGIN!!

More Adventures COMING SOON...

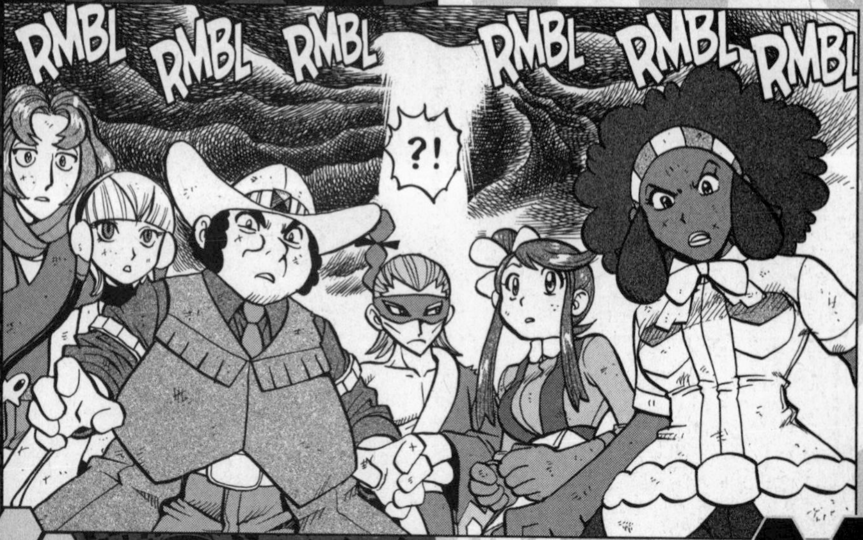
RMBL RMBL RMBL
RMBL RMBL RMBL
?!

Team Plasma launches an all-out attack on the Nacrene Museum to steal the mysterious Dark Stone and summon powerful Legendary Pokemon Zekrom! Opposing them is the full might of the Unova Gym Leaders—plus lowly trainer Black... *Who will prevail?!*

WILL BLACK TURN OUT TO BE A HELP...OR A HINDRANCE?

Plus, meet Swanna, Unfezant, Lilligant, Cryogonal, Tornadus, Landorus, and Larvesta!

VOL. 11 AVAILABLE AUGUST 2013!

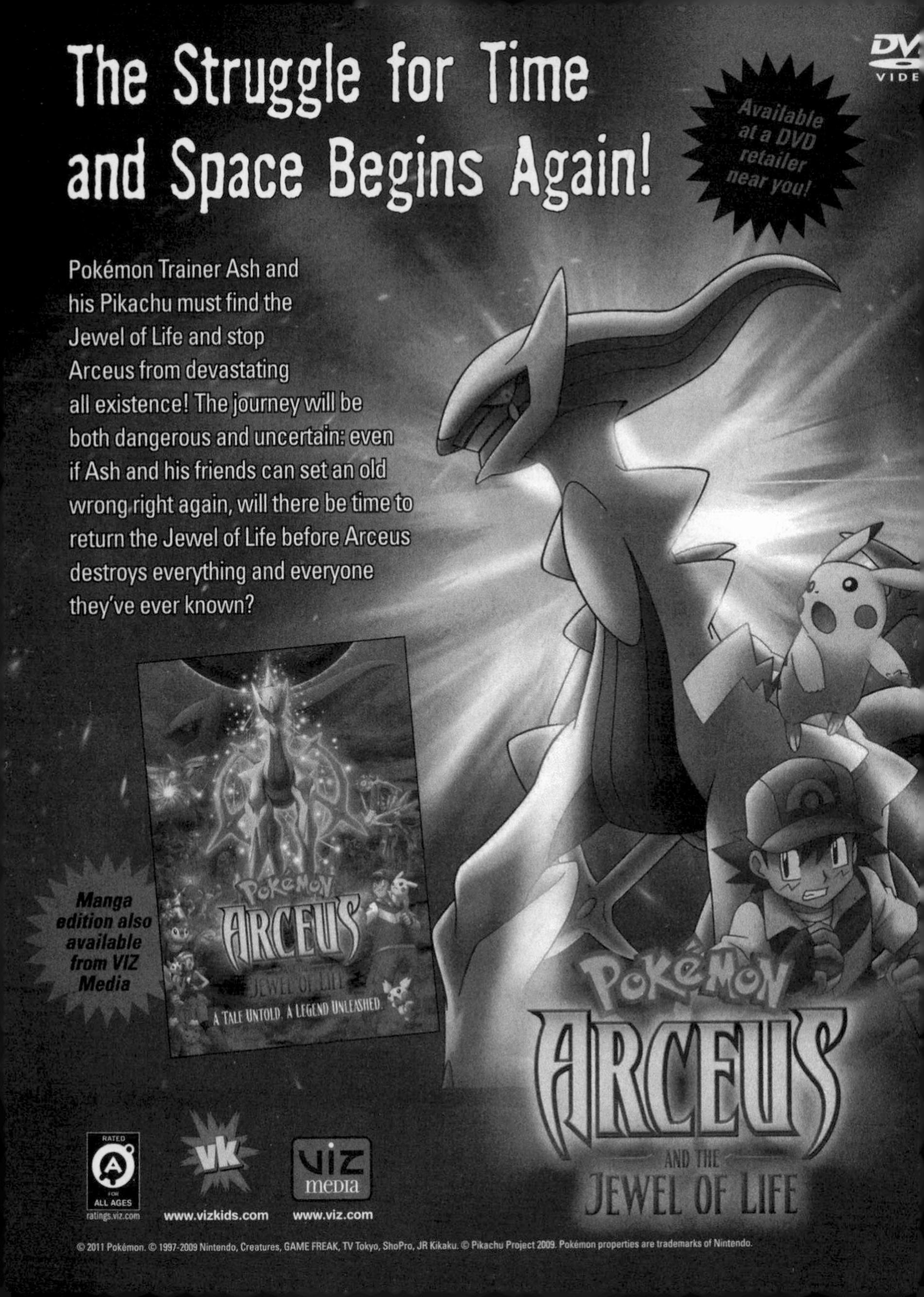
The Struggle for Time and Space Begins Again!
Available at a DVD retailer near you!
Pokémon Trainer Ash and his Pikachu must find the Jewel of Life and stop Arceus from devastating all existence! The journey will be both dangerous and uncertain: even if Ash and his friends can set an old wrong right again, will there be time to return the Jewel of Life before Arceus destroys everything and everyone they've ever known?
Manga edition also available from VIZ Media
Pokémon Arceus and the Jewel of Life
A Tale Untold, A Legend Unleashed.
Pokémon Arceus and the Jewel of Life
RATED A FOR ALL AGES
ratings.viz.com
www.vizkids.com
viz media
www.viz.com
© 2011 Pokémon. © 1997-2009 Nintendo, Creatures, GAME FREAK, TV Tokyo, ShoPro, JR Kikaku. © Pikachu Project 2009. Pokémon properties are trademarks of Nintendo.

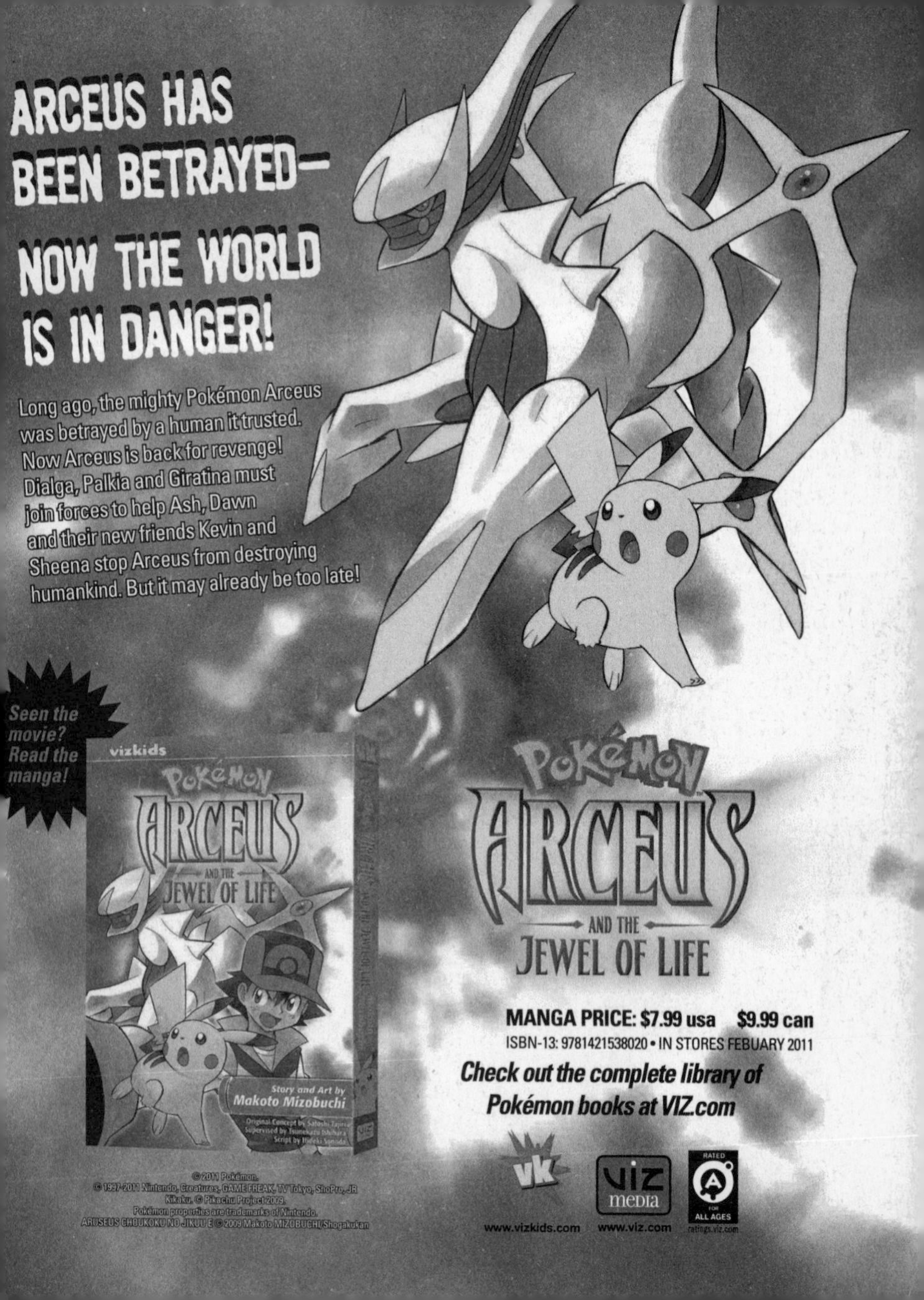
ARCEUS HAS BEEN BETRAYED—
NOW THE WORLD IS IN DANGER!
Long ago, the mighty Pokémon Arceus was betrayed by a human it trusted. Now Arceus is back for revenge! Dialga, Palkia and Giratina must join forces to help Ash, Dawn and their new friends Kevin and Sheena stop Arceus from destroying humankind. But it may already be too late!
Seen the movie? Read the manga!
vizkids
Pokémon
Arceus
AND THE
Jewel of Life
Story and Art by
Makoto Mizobuchi
Original Concept by Satoshi Tajiri
Supervised by Tsunekazu Ishihara
Script by Hideki Sonoda
Pokémon
Arceus
AND THE
Jewel of Life
MANGA PRICE: $7.99 usa $9.99 can
ISBN-13: 9781421538020 • IN STORES FEBUARY 2011
Check out the complete library of Pokémon books at VIZ.com
© 2011 Pokémon.
© 1997-2011 Nintendo, Creatures, GAME FREAK, TV Tokyo, ShoPro, JR Kikaku. © Pikachu Project 2009.
Pokémon properties are trademarks of Nintendo.
ARUSEUS CHOUKOKU NO JIKUU E © 2009 Makoto MIZOBUCHI/Shogakukan
vk
VIZ media
RATED A FOR ALL AGES
www.vizkids.com
www.viz.com
ratings.viz.com

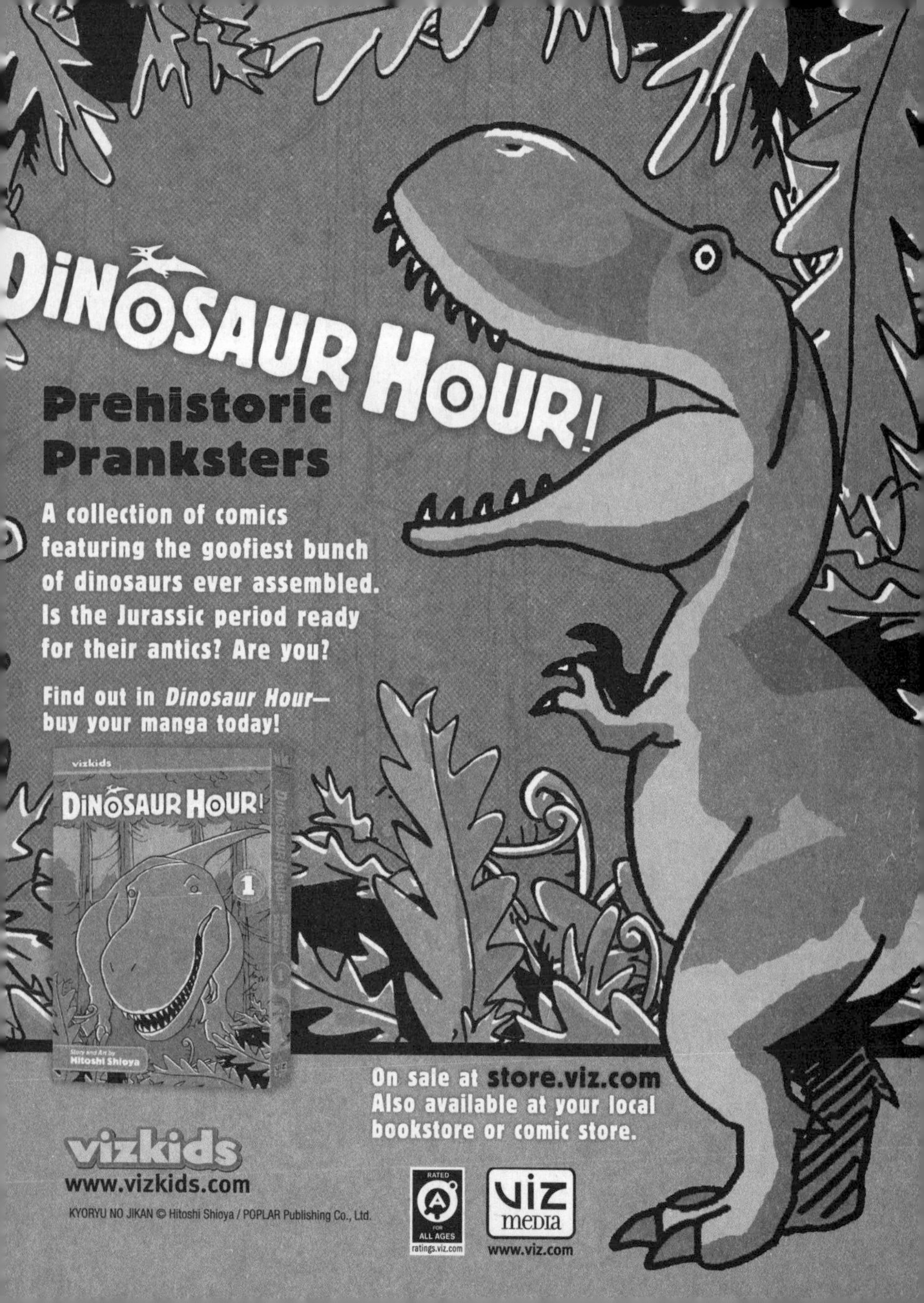
DINOSAUR HOUR!
Prehistoric Pranksters
A collection of comics featuring the goofiest bunch of dinosaurs ever assembled. Is the Jurassic period ready for their antics? Are you?
Find out in *Dinosaur Hour*—buy your manga today!
vizkids
DINOSAUR HOUR!
1
Story and Art by Hitoshi Shioya
On sale at store.viz.com
Also available at your local bookstore or comic store.
vizkids
www.vizkids.com
KYORYU NO JIKAN © Hitoshi Shioya / POPLAR Publishing Co., Ltd.
RATED A FOR ALL AGES
ratings.viz.com
VIZ media
www.viz.com

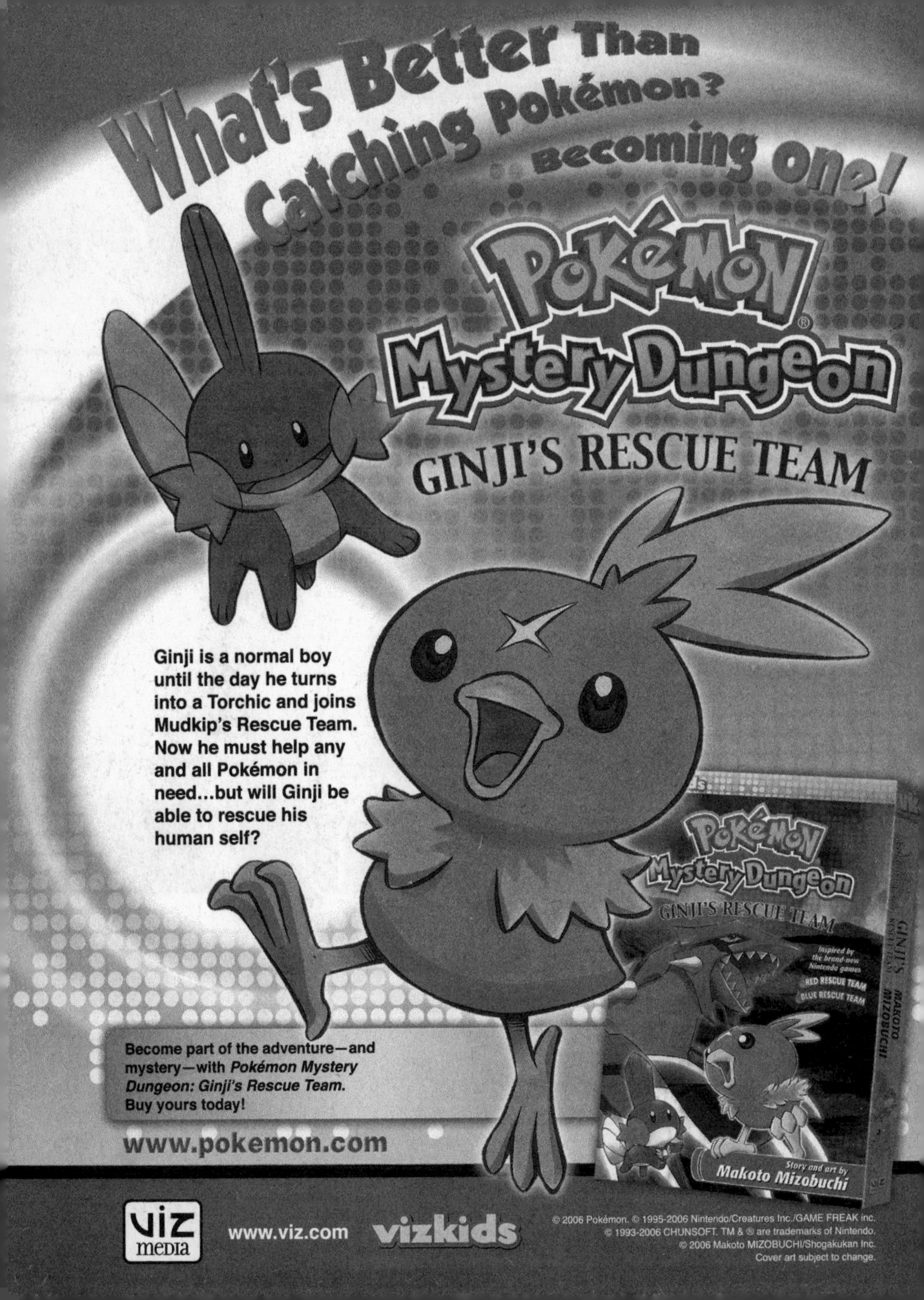

What's Better Than Catching Pokémon?
Becoming one!
Pokémon® Mystery Dungeon
GINJI'S RESCUE TEAM
Ginji is a normal boy until the day he turns into a Torchic and joins Mudkip's Rescue Team. Now he must help any and all Pokémon in need...but will Ginji be able to rescue his human self?
Pokémon Mystery Dungeon
GINJI'S RESCUE TEAM
Inspired by the brand-new Nintendo games
RED RESCUE TEAM
BLUE RESCUE TEAM
Story and art by
Makoto Mizobuchi
Become part of the adventure—and mystery—with *Pokémon Mystery Dungeon: Ginji's Rescue Team.* Buy yours today!
www.pokemon.com
viz media
www.viz.com
vizkids
© 2006 Pokémon. © 1995-2006 Nintendo/Creatures Inc./GAME FREAK inc.
© 1993-2006 CHUNSOFT. TM & ® are trademarks of Nintendo.
© 2006 Makoto MIZOBUCHI/Shogakukan Inc.
Cover art subject to change.

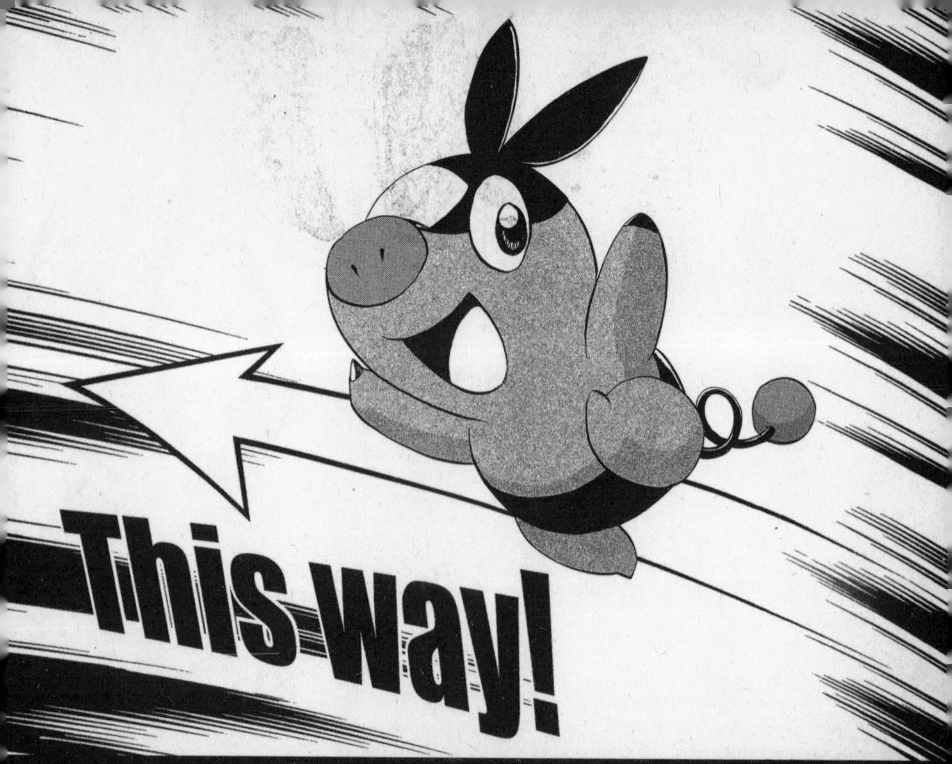
This way!

THIS IS THE END OF THIS GRAPHIC NOVEL!

To properly enjoy this VIZ Media graphic novel, please turn it around and begin reading from right to left.

This book has been printed in the original Japanese format in order to preserve the orientation of the original artwork. Have fun with it!

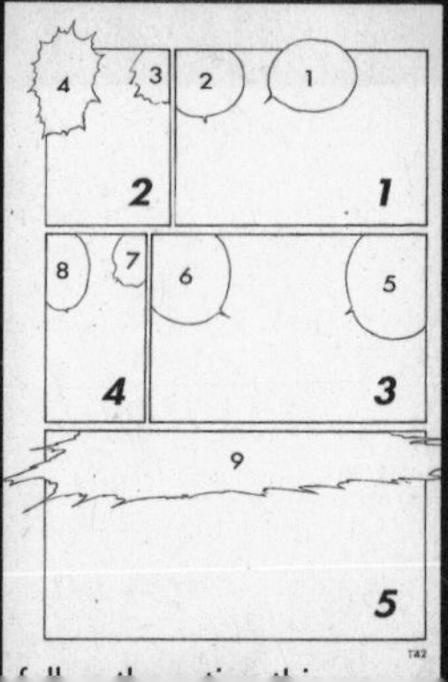
1
2
1
3
4
2
5
6
3
7
8
4
9
5